Coffee, Anyone?

Book 1

Coffee, Anyone?

Amy Courter

CHAPTER 1
Amber

"Man, I am going to be late again!" I muttered under my breath as I pulled up next for my turn at Starbucks to get my daily caramel double espresso. I inched forward after paying $8.59 for my drink. Taking my first huge, craved gulp of the hot liquid I pulled into traffic. "Ah…now that's more like it," I said out loud with a contented sigh.

I had just dumped off my "new-to-me" teen-aged daughter, Sophie, at the high school. Her dad, Joshua, grounded her AGAIN. And then he is away for a week at a time, and I "get" to carry out the punishment. "That's just GREAT," I grumbled through gritted teeth. Things were finally getting a little better between Sophie and me until this last grounding and then everything went to hell in a handbasket. I'm new to the stepmother gig so I guess I don't get a say in the rules and regulations around here, I thought grumpily.

Coffee, Anyone?

Exactly three months ago on June 1st, I married Joshua Alan Jackson and became a stepmom to Sophie. She is not a bad girl; she's a teen. I think Josh sometimes forgets the things HE did when he was a teen. Josh is a Special Forces Private Investigator for the government and travels a LOT. Since our two-week honeymoon to a resort in Denver, Colorado (in which we took Sophie along), he has been home exactly 14 days total. "I guess this is what I signed up for, though," I sighed out loud. If only Sophie could have social media and/or her computer when she is grounded to her room, at least she could see what was going on with her friends. Sophie seemed to be finally coming out of her shell a couple of weeks ago after the sudden death of her mom, Denise, last year.

I suppose Sophie thinks I am trying to replace her mom now that I am married to her dad. When Josh and I married, he did put away MOST of the pictures of Denise in the house, although Sophie kept her mom's picture in her bedroom. That's okay, though, Denise is/was Sophie's mom. I don't know if she will ever call ME "mom" but if I can at least get her to look at me without quite so much disgust and hate, that would be very nice for sure.

Amy Courter

Josh thinks, because he is a private detective and sometimes works under cover, that all of us need to keep our family pics off social media so nobody can see his face and family. Sophie and I have explicit directions to NEVER post a picture of our family on Facebook or email. Josh says he doesn't want to take any chances with his family not being safe. I guess we just need to suck it up and realize it is for our own good.

I chuckled as I thought of my profile picture on Facebook; it's Fred, Sophie's beloved fat cat (by himself). I swear Fred hates me. Every time I walk upstairs to put clothes away or make the beds, Fred takes a swipe at my ankle as I am walking up the stairs. Believe me—I have the scabs and scars as evidence! And then to prove he hates me, Fred pees on my stuff no matter where I put it.

The last time Josh was home he told Sophie to quit feeding Fred so much and making him fat. I almost burst out laughing but contained myself. I have been feeding Fred ham—lots of it! Fred LOVES it, but still hates ME. I throw the ham at Fred, so he won't claw me when I'm going up and down the stairs. Sometimes I forget to take "my ammunition" with me to distract Fred and he ALWAYS seems to be lurking and ready to attack at least one ankle on the stairway. I am thinking ham can't be too good for Fred, so maybe I won't have to put up with him for long!

Coffee, Anyone?

I really would like to get a smallish dog at the rescue place in town. I have been watching their advertisements and most of the dogs have been the large ones. I guess it doesn't matter since Josh doesn't want another animal in the house, so I guess I'm stuck with Fred until he (Fred, not Josh--ha-ha!) expires.

I am very fortunate to have been able to transfer my position of hotel manager in the Des Moines, IA hotel to the Fort Dodge, IA hotel without losing any seniority, pay, or benefits. Des Moines *Visitors Matter* is where I first met Josh—we are located near the Des Moines airport and while Josh was waiting for his lift to the airport, we met for the first time. He often spends the night before his flight at our Des Moines hotel to avoid leaving his home in the middle of the night to catch an early morning flight out. After we met that first time, Josh always made a point to stop in my office to say, "Hello, Amber, how are you?" before catching his flight or after getting off his flight since I usually worked 10-hour days and was in my office.

Amy Courter

Soon we got together for a real date, and it seemed like we were made for each other. It was a whirlwind romance I must admit, but I was smitten, and when he wanted me to move in with him and his daughter I told him, "No, not until we are married." Josh said, "Well, let's get married then!" As I look back at our short courtship now, I wonder if Josh just needed a "jailer" for his teenaged daughter. Stop it! I tell myself. I know Josh loves me. He just seemed to show it more before we got married.

I suppose that is the complaint of most married couples as I think about my friend and co-worker at the Fort Dodge hotel, Maggie. She and I like to talk smack about our hubs when we go out for a coffee or lunch. Sometimes Maggie and Bob have dinner out with Josh and me, but it has been a long while since that has happened. Mental note to self: talk to Josh about dinner out again with Maggie & Bob.

Thankfully, after moving to Fort Dodge, IA and taking on the hotel manager position, I was able to cut my hours down to coincide with Sophie's school hours, so that works very well. On the way to Fort Dodge Senior High to pick up Sophie, I was trying to think what I had in the freezer/cupboard/refrigerator that could make a decent meal that Sophie would like.

Coffee, Anyone?

At 3:30 as Sophie slid into my sea foam green Prius, I asked her how her day went. She grunted something (not sure exactly what) as she buckled her seat belt. I told her about my day and a rude customer that I had the privilege of meeting that morning. Sophie was not impressed or interested.

As we pulled into our driveway, I asked Sophie if mac & cheese sounded good. She said, "Fine." That was one good thing about not having a man around for every meal — our grocery bill was very reasonable since neither Sophie, nor I were crazy about meat. We loved our cheeses, crackers, and vegetables, though, as well as DESSERT!

Sophie was on the swim team at Fort Dodge Senior High and there was a swim meet tomorrow after school. The coach usually gave the team the day before a meet off so they could rest up for the meet. I have never heard of that before. It must work well, however, as the team is very good.

***

As I watched from the stands, I was impressed with Sophie's flawless underwater turn and swift dolphin kick back to her stroke, the butterfly. She is a natural at swimming. Shaking my head, I thought, Josh, you should be here. You are missing all of this and soon Sophie will be grown and gone, and you will have missed something you can never get back. Sigh.

Amy Courter

Luckily, I had the time to pick up fresh fruit and veggies for the week after dropping Sophie off for a short warm up before the swim meet. Now we are set for the week, I think, unless "tall, dark, and handsome" comes home for the weekend. I shrugged, thinking, I will cross that bridge when I get to it. Often, Josh doesn't tell me when to expect him home, he just shows up or doesn't. It's hard to be prepared food-wise when he doesn't let me know, but I guess I should just count my blessings instead of being annoyed.

I have asked Josh what exactly he does each day and of course it is *classified,* and he cannot tell me. I have never met anyone that works with Josh, and I would really like to do that. We wives could commiserate with each other regarding our hubs' schedules.

I googled Josh after I first met him when he told me his name. There sure wasn't much on social media about him. It didn't have anything about his line of work. I told him later that I could find very little about him on the internet and he said, "Good! That's the way I want it! I avoid social media like the plague!" I guess that makes sense why there is so little information out there about him. He is happy to fly under the radar, especially with his *confidential* job.

Coffee, Anyone?

It looks like Sophie is up on the block for the freestyle. Sophie has a beautiful stroke gliding through the water like a fish, appearing to expend minimal effort, even though she has pulled ahead to the leader position. "Go, Sophie, GO!" I yell from the crowded stands of parents and families. That's another first place ribbon for Sophie today! I should have made a video of it for her dad, but I didn't think of it in time.

As I wait in the stands for Sophie to get dried off and changed, I am still shaking my head over her last grounding and frankly feel sorry for her. Even though Josh won't like it because he is the "we must save our pennies" type of guy, I ask Sophie when she finally emerges from the locker room, "Hey, we need to celebrate your victories; you did so well in your races! How about grabbing a bite to eat at your favorite place, Tropical Smoothie?"

Sophie smiled (kind of) and said, "Sure!"

I sure wish Josh could have seen her swim tonight; he would have been so very proud of his girl. Regionals are coming up in a couple of weeks, then state the following week and swimming competition will soon be over, so I am hoping Josh will get home for at least one of the upcoming meets.

Amy Courter

Chapter 2
Sophie

I hate my life, I thought as I turned up the volume on my AirPods to listen to my favorite song, "Drivers License" by Olivia Rodrigo. It's bad enough that my mom died last year and now I am forced to put up with my dad's new wife and she doesn't have a clue about anything. Dad is gone almost all the time but before he leaves for his extended trips, he manages to ground me for SOMETHING that isn't even my fault. Okay, maybe it wasn't very "mature" what my friend Lindsey and I did, but it didn't actually HURT anyone. All we did is *67 and call random numbers in the phone book so they wouldn't know who the caller was. It was awesome, actually! Lindsey and I took turns with variants of: "Is your refrigerator running?" Waiting for an answer, then we would shout: "Well, ya better go catch it then!" Ha-ha! I still am laughing!

Coffee, Anyone?

Well, somehow, one of the "pranked" figured out who we were and here I am, stuck in my room for a week with no computer and no phone. That's a bit harsh I am thinking. Mom would not have enforced Dad's punishment after he left for work. That's just the way it worked around here, although I know she took some heat for not enforcing the punishment Dad doled out. When he got home and figured out that I had my phone and computer all week (his favorite things to remove from my room), there was lots of yelling between the two of them. I just closed my door, turned up my AirPods volume and listened to "Déjà Vu". At least he didn't ground me from my favorite singer Olivia Rodrigo's music. Their fights got especially bad the month before she died and when Dad left for the week, I found Mom crying in the bathroom. I felt kind of responsible for always being the screw up, but I guess that's what I do best, sorry to say.

***

Amy Courter

I met Lindsey at a cool church Amber and I have been attending on Sunday nights after Dad leaves for work. Lindsey and her mom, Rachel are really cool, and I like being with them. Amber usually lets me spend as much time as I want with Lindsey. She thinks Lindsey is a good influence on me! I had to fib and tell Amber and Dad that I was the one who made the prank phone calls, or they would not have let me hang out with Lindsey again—I know how their minds work. Lindsey was so sorry I got in trouble, but at least I still get to see and talk to her on Sundays and during lunch at school. She really listens to me and doesn't interrupt me or tell me I'm stupid for thinking what I think, and when she swears not to tell a living, breathing soul, I believe her and feel safe sharing my secrets with her.

Mom never met Lindsey or her mom, Rachel. She would have liked them both I think. I miss my mom so much. I wish my dad would have died instead of my mom. I know I shouldn't think that, but it's the way I feel. My dad does not understand me and doesn't even try to talk to me. He just barks orders and then leaves. My mom never missed a swimming meet, and my dad seems to care less whether I swim fast or swim at all!

Coffee, Anyone?

At least Amber comes to watch me swim at my swim meets. I could even hear her cheering for me at my last meet and then she took me to my favorite place to celebrate afterwards. I guess Amber isn't so bad, but I wish she wouldn't treat me like a prisoner. I suppose she would get into trouble, too, though, if she let me off the hook from my dad's grounding like my mom did. I overheard Amber trying to tell Dad that he was being too strict with me and pushing me further and further away from them by being so harsh, but he wouldn't listen.

I heard Dad tell Amber, "Don't question me! I know what is best for my daughter and you don't, especially since you don't have any children of your own." I heard Amber sniffing, as Dad walked away. I snuck back to my room and put my covers over my head.

***

"Amber, I see Lindsey—I'm going to go over there and sit by her, okay?"

"Sure, honey, that is fine, but don't giggle and talk too much during the sermon, okay?" Amber asked with raised eyebrows.

Amy Courter

I gave Amber the thumbs up and squealed while hugging my bestie, Lindsey! I really love coming to this church and am so glad Amber found it for us! We have youth group after the Sunday night service while the parents sit and visit over coffee. Dad and Mom never took me to church, and I have learned so much that I never knew!

I did ask Dad one time why he and mom never took me to church or went themselves, and he started an argument with Amber asking her why she was taking me to church and filling my head with all these ideas, so I never brought it up again and we don't talk about church in front of Dad.

Coffee, Anyone?

One thing I learned from church is that God doesn't make junk and He even knows how many hairs are on my head! I can't remember the Bible verses like Lindsey does, but I remember the gist of what our youth pastor said. I had never heard of Salvation before and what it meant. There is a whole lot I don't understand but I am listening. The only scripture I know is the salvation verse, John 3:16, "God so loved the world that He gave His only Son so that all who believe in Him will not perish but have ever lasting life". I am still trying to figure out the depth of this passage and Lindsey is very helpful. She makes it all sound so easy and simple and asks me why I don't just ask Jesus to come and live in my heart and believe, but I keep reminding her that she has known this stuff for years and I am hearing it for the first time EVER. I want to know exactly what this means before I commit to anything.

***

Amy Courter

After Mom died, the police came to our house and asked Dad to come to the police station with them because they had some questions for him. Dad told me it was very common for the police to first suspect the husband in a sudden death of his wife, and it was nothing for me to worry about. Well, I did worry. I also started watching Dad intensely and noticed that he did not seem very upset about Mom dying. I didn't even see him cry; he just kept pecking away on his stupid phone. Could Dad have murdered Mom?!? I can't believe I am asking myself this, but this is definitely messed up.

Last year in junior high, one of my best friends (at the time) or so I thought, was Beth. I was so angry and sad about Mom's death and my dad's ability to appear like nothing was wrong that I told her about the police coming to my house to get my dad and taking him away in the police car. I thought she understood that this was something I didn't want everyone to know. I told Beth my terrible thoughts about thinking maybe my dad killed my mom. She hugged me and told me everything was going to be okay and acted like she loved me and totally had my back, but three weeks later when I went back to school, I was opening my locker and Jody, a girl I don't really like because she is a big gossip, said that everyone at school thinks my dad killed my mom! I could not believe Beth would do this to me. I thought Beth and I were great friends and I thought I could trust her.

Coffee, Anyone?

 I turned around sprinted down the hall and out of the school and when I was out of energy to run, I walked. I walked around a long while going nowhere in particular, just sobbing uncontrollably with snot running down my face. Finally, when I had drained myself of all emotion, I walked home. Dad was waiting for me. The school had already called him and told him I ran out of the school visibly upset about something.

"Sophie, honey, what is going on? I thought you agreed to go to school today. What changed?" my dad asked.

"I couldn't handle it, Dad—it was just too hard. Everyone was looking at me and it made me tear up and cry and I didn't want to do it in front of everyone," I said, telling the partial truth.

"Well, you need to buck up, Soph—you have to go back to school someday—you might as well get it over with."

"Dad, you are not like me, and I need more time to wrap my head around what happened to Mom. I can't just go on with my life. I need some answers. Why did this happen?" I cried.

Amy Courter

I could tell Dad was thinking over what I just said. I didn't tell him the complete truth, but some of it was true.

"Honey, I am sad, too, about your mom's death but you can't let it just shut you down and keep you from going forward in life."

"You don't seem to be so sad, Dad, and what did the police say to you when you went to the station? You wouldn't tell me anything and I need to know!" I yelled.

"I didn't realize you were still curious about that, sweetheart. I told you that they just wanted to talk to me and then they brought me home. No big deal. They were just looking into all possibilities regarding your mom's death. But, since you seem to be concerned about the police visit, I will tell you that they called this morning after doing an autopsy on Mom and conceded there was no foul play," my dad informed me.

"What does THAT mean?" I asked.

Coffee, Anyone?

"No foul play means they think Mom died from a severe anaphylactic peanut reaction, and the investigator was satisfied with his examination, saying the peanut oil could have come from anywhere in the house since she had dumped out her purse and seemed to be rifling through it for her EpiPen," Dad said. "In other words, the police do not think someone killed Mom; her allergy of peanuts was the killer."

"Oh," I said trying to think if I should apologize to Dad for thinking he killed Mom, but decided not to since he, hopefully, didn't know that I was thinking that, unless he hears from school parents because of Beth's big mouth!
"But, Dad, we are always so careful about not buying anything with peanuts in it, so how could Mom have come in contact with peanuts? I don't understand!"

"We may never know, honey. We can't bring Mom back and we just need to accept that she is gone now and put one step in front of the other, going forward."
I sadly nodded and said, "I guess."

Amy Courter

"Sophie, I need to be back at work on Monday, so I will give you another two days at home—how does that sound? But today and tomorrow we need to be thinking of who can pick you up and take you to school and come and get you after swim team practice? I put a discreet ad in the paper last week to see if I can find someone able and willing to come and live with us for a while and take care of these things. In the meantime, should I call your friend, Beth's parents and ask them if you can stay there for a week or so?"

"NO! I do NOT want to stay at Beth's!" I spat, leaving my dad bewildered by my outburst.

"Okay, fine. But we do need to figure this out, Soph. Just be thinking."

I didn't want to think about who would do the things my mom used to do for me when Dad wasn't around, which was most of the time. I just wanted to go back in time and reboot and have a do-over of my life in general. I hate this. Why can't Dad just let me do me and he can do him?

***

Coffee, Anyone?

Things are somewhat better now that we have Amber. At least I don't have to listen to my neighbor "Nosie Nellie" anymore. My dad came up with this "brilliant" (in his opinion) idea after Mom died that our nosie neighbor, Nellie, should come and stay with me while he was out of town. She was WAAAY worse than Amber ever could be! And she was always quizzing me about my dad—did he like this or do you think he will like that? Nellie and my mom used to have coffee together sometimes so dad said he thought Mom would like it that we asked Nellie to come over and help us.

Mom told me once that Nellie is divorced with no children of her own and works from home. Mom always felt sorry for Nellie and thought Nellie's biggest problem was that she was lonely with nobody to look after. Nosie Nellie got all weird when Dad and Amber got engaged, like she was mad about it or something. Creepy. Maybe Nosie Nellie thought she could get my dad to marry HER! As If! I guess she is probably not that old, but she is definitely not my dad's type. I found Nosie Nellie standing in our kitchen a couple days after Mom died with a coffee can in her hands. I must have freaked her out because she acted really guilty like she had done something suspicious. She said she had loaned some coffee to my mom and needed it back. Whatever.

Amy Courter

My swim team peeps (especially the boys on the team) keep telling me that Amber is HOT. I had not really thought of Amber in that way. I guess she is kind of pretty. I think she said she is 37 and Dad is 42. Amber is pretty stylish, too. She doesn't wear jeans that are out of style like Mom used to wear. When I confronted Mom once about her "mom jeans" she just laughed and said, "Well, what do you expect—I'm a mom!" I guess Mom would be in style today if she were still alive, since Mom jeans are BACK! Ha!

Amber has great hair, too. It's blonde and shoulder length and she is always doing something interesting and fun with it. She offered to try some of it on my hair, but I said no. I don't want to act too friendly to the "enemy." Although, I guess she is not the enemy. She is just trying to please Dad and do what he wants her to do. My life is so messed up. I don't see it getting better until I'm 18 and can move out on my own.

Coffee, Anyone?

Chapter 3
Amber

Josh still hasn't called me—it's been two days. Whenever I call him, it goes directly to voice mail and if I text him, he texts back, "I'm busy—not now." I know Josh has a lot of responsibility and has an important job to do, but would it kill him to talk to me for five minutes!?

I need a distraction. "Hello, Nikki? This is Amber. Is this a good time to talk a few minutes?"

"Sure, hi, Amber! What's up?"

"Oh, you know, married life is just kind of sucky and I'm trying to get my mind off of it and thought I'd see how things are going there in Des Moines to distract myself," I said trying to sound more upbeat than I was feeling.

Laughing out loud, Nikki replied, "Isn't the romantic Josh still bringing you flowers and candy like he did when you worked here in Des Moines at *Visitors Matter*?"

Amy Courter

"Heck no, and I don't require flowers and candy, but I WOULD like to hear from the man every now and then. Do you have a funny guest story you can tell me to take my mind off my problems for a couple minutes?"

"As a matter of fact, I do," said Nikki playfully. "I will tell you one, and then you will have to reciprocate with one of your wonderful stories about YOUR guests there in Fort Dodge, Iowa!"

"Deal!" I said enthusiastically since Nikki was such a great storyteller and her stories were ALWAYS better than mine! Or maybe she embellished to make them sound that way, but either way, I enjoyed the heck out of them!

"Okay, here goes. Last week one of our guests left me a nasty note on the *Visitors Matter* website saying her spa treatment was an awful experience and the masseuse didn't know what she was doing. She said she had bruises all over her body from the overzealous treatment and she could hardly even move afterwards. She ended her posting by saying our hotel would hear from her lawyer."

"Oh my gosh! What did you do?" I gasped.

Coffee, Anyone?

"Oh, I went back through the spa logbook to find out who it might have been on that day and talked to the masseuse who would have done the massage. I got the masseuse's story and then called the woman."

"Was she still mad and would she talk to you?" I asked.

"Oh yeah, she was willing to talk, and she listened too. I asked her if she knew what a deep tissue massage was and she said, no. I asked her if she asked the masseuse to stop at any time and again, she said no. Then she added, "but she should have known with all my groaning and screaming that I was not liking it!"

"Oh boy," I remarked, fully intent on the outcome.

"Oh boy, is right! Then I asked her if she would like to come back to the hotel spa as my guest and have a regular massage at her convenience. She said she would and that she really just wanted someone to rub her back."

Laughing, I said, "Wow, Nikki, you are so good and are always thinking how to make things better for everyone! You just saved the hotel from a possible lawsuit! Plus, you pulled me out of my funk with your delightful story-telling ability."

Amy Courter

"I know, but you are probably the only one who knows I am good since you have done this job yourself," Nikki chuckles, "You are great for my ego and I'm glad I could help put you in a better state of mind! Now it's your turn—lay one of your guest stories on me!"

"Uh oh, duty calls," I laughed, "I will have to get back to you another time with my story! Hey, before we hang up, help me brainstorm about putting a Starbucks in our hotels next time we talk! Bye, bye, doll!"

My ex-coworker and replacement, Nikki, at the Des Moines hotel is such a gem. I sure hope the rest of the staff there appreciates her like I do. The transition from me to Nikki in the management position was seamless due to Nikki's ability to quickly grasp and comprehend my training enabling her to hit the ground running in her new position as manager of the hotel.

I hang up with a grin on my face as I ask the next customer, "Hello, how can I help you?"

***

"Hey, how's it going?" Josh asks as I pick up the phone.

"Hi, it's good to finally hear from you. I was getting worried," I say with concern.

Coffee, Anyone?

"Now why would you worry, Amber? I told you I was working on something important this week and wouldn't be able to talk much."

"I know, Josh, but it's been two days with hardly a word from you! When will you be home?"

"Not this weekend, I'm sorry to say. We are still in the throes of this important case, and it is just not feasible for me to come home right now. I promise, though, next week to make it a priority to get home," Josh says.

"Fine," I say with venom. "We need to talk."

I toss my phone on the counter feeling uncertain about a lot of things, trust being the biggest issue. Could Josh me messing around on me?

***

I am so thankful for the school calendar, so I know what is going on in Sophie's world. I noticed there is a school dance coming up shortly. Also, one of the boys at youth group is evidently crushing on Sophie. Bradley's mom, Tina, asked me how I would feel if Bradley would ask Sophie to go to the school dance with him. I briefly thought about telling Tina I needed to first talk to Sophie's dad and would get back to her; instead, I said, "I think that is wonderful if Bradley would like to ask Sophie to go to the school dance!"

Amy Courter

Josh has never met Bradley or Tina or anyone else that attends our church. The only time Sophie brought up the church we have been attending, Josh went ballistic. He told me he was a Christian when we were dating. Maybe he just THINKS he is a Christian. I feel he wants Sophie (and me!) to just sit at home alone and not meet or interact with others. I know Sophie feels "jailed" sometimes and I am beginning to feel that way, too. I think that is why I was defiant and didn't wait to check with Josh about Sophie going to the dance with Bradley if he gets up the nerve to ask her. I will tell Josh next time he calls IF he calls.

***

Bradley DID get up the nerve and asked Sophie to the school dance! She was so cute when she came to me and asked if she could go. She said Bradley's mom would be driving them there. Then she said, "I was wondering if you could help me with my hair before the dance?"

"Absolutely!" I said with enthusiasm. "Sophie, I haven't cleared all this with your dad yet, but I saw on the school news calendar that they need adult chaperones for the dance. Would you be okay with me volunteering for that? I think it might help your case for wanting to go to the dance."

I could tell Sophie was pondering this very carefully. She finally said, "Okay, but you aren't going to follow us around at the dance, right?"

Coffee, Anyone?

"Only if you aren't where you should be," I promised with glee in my eyes.

"Oh, brother…." Sophie mumbled as she left the room.

"Hey, Sophie," I called out in order to get her to come back and talk some more, "I thought maybe we could go shopping for a new dress for the dance for you Saturday? Your dad won't be home this weekend and it would be a good time for us to go."

"I would love that!" Sophie replied big-eyed.

"Do you have any idea of what kind of dresses girls are wearing to the school dances?" I asked.

"No, but I will take a look at some of the girls' pictures on Instagram and I saw some dresses on the girls' snap stories, too, uh…if I can have my computer back?" Sophie asked.

"Tell you what, let me get my computer and we can look together," I smiled.

***

Holy buckets, I thought to myself as I looked at the price tag! I had no idea what they were asking for a homecoming dress these days.

Amy Courter

"I really like this one, Amber," Sophie said as she was looking at herself in the Macy's store mirror.

"I do, too, honey, but…" I said as I flipped over the price tag so Sophie could see it.
"Yikes!" Sophie whispered.

"Let's look around a little more to see if there is anything you like that is a little more reasonable in price, okay?" I said with more enthusiasm than I felt.

"Okay," Sophie said quietly.

We shopped and we shopped, and we shopped some more, going in one store after another in Des Moines. I knew my way around, luckily, after living there for several years. I just thought of a store we had not yet tried.

"Sophie, what will you do with your dress after the dance? Will you ever wear it again, do you think?" I asked.

"Probably not, most girls don't," Sophie answered honestly.

"I might have the perfect solution then!" I grinned as I turned down Grand Ave.

Coffee, Anyone?

We stepped inside the trendy shop, eyeing dress after dress that were just plain adorable! I got excited as Sophie and I started browsing through the dresses and looking at the price tags. Sophie asked, "How can these dresses be so cheap and also so cute?"

As the store manager came out of her office, she stopped in her tracks and said, "Amber!" She opened her arms for a hug, and I hugged her back enthusiastically.

"Are you back in Des Moines now?" Muriel asked.

"No, just shopping with...my daughter, Sophie," I cautiously said while eyeing Sophie for any attitude of me calling her my daughter. "She is going to the homecoming dance and needs something beautiful to match her beauty!"

Sophie looked a little embarrassed, but I could tell she was also pleased to hear me say that she was beautiful (although she is).

Muriel said, "Come with me. We just got something in I think Sophie will ADORE."

As we followed Muriel to the back of the store, I winked at Sophie, and she grinned ear to ear.

Amy Courter

"OH. MY. GOSH," Sophie exclaimed as she twirled around in the gorgeous dress. "I think I like this one better than the $400 dress from Macy's!"

"Me too and look at the price tag! Only a fourth of the price!"

"But, Amber, I don't understand. There has to be a catch…doesn't there?" Sophie asked with a confused look on her face.

"There is a catch, it's called 'renting' rather than 'buying'. And if that is okay with you, that's what we will do. We simply pay the rental price now and come back to pick up the dress the day before the event and return it within three days after the event."

Muriel chimed in saying, "Amber, for you and your daughter, I will let you take the dress now. I don't want to take the chance of someone else trying it on and ripping it or getting make up on it." I looked at Muriel with unspoken gratitude.

"It's VERY okay with me, Amber! I love it! Lindsey told me at school yesterday she had some sandals she wore to her aunt's wedding last year that she outgrew and that I can have them if they fit me! They will go perfect with the dress!"

Coffee, Anyone?

"Well, let's pay for your dress and go to lunch!" I said happily and we practically skipped to the cash register.

"That was so much fun, Amber, thank you so much," Sophie said with tears in her eyes as we started for home.

"You are so very welcome, Sophie," I smiled quietly.

"This was the best day EVER," sighed Sophie contentedly.

I had to fast blink to stop a tear or two and nodded my head in agreement.

***

"Tina, I hear you are driving Bradley and Sophie to the homecoming dance in a few weeks," I said as I found Tina at church after the Sunday evening service. As we sat down for coffee while the youth group met, I said, "I saw on the school's website that they were looking for adult chaperones for the school dance and I have Sophie's permission to volunteer. Would you like to do that with me?"

"I'd love to!" Tina replied with a smile. "I will be driving the kids there and back anyway so why not?"

Amy Courter

Rachel, Lindsey's mom, joined us with her cup of coffee and said while laughing, "The kids just told me that the three of them are going to the dance together: Lindsey, Bradley and Sophie! Quite the date, huh?"

We all laughed together and then Rachel said, "Amber, Sophie told Lindsey about this chic little shop where you bought her dress. Can you give me the address?"

"I sure can, and tell Muriel that 'Amber sent you'," I said with a very pleased nod.

***

I take off an hour early on Tuesdays to attend my Pilates class at the downtown studio. As I was changing for my hourly workout, I recalled Sophie's question last week when I told her I would pick her up after my Pilates class. She asked, "What does Pilates actually do for you?"

I told her, "Well, Pilates helps me remember to breathe deeply and to walk with a purpose, a straight back and not slump. It strengthens and tones my muscles, it has helped me with flexibility and coordination, too. It also quiets my soul, along with God. Would you like to go with me sometime?"

Sophie looked thoughtful and said, "If Pilates can do all that for ME, sure, why not?"

Coffee, Anyone?

Her answer made me smile and I thought I should see if Rachel and Lindsey would want to come with us sometime and make it a date.

***

Josh called tonight. I decided I should tell him about the school dance and Sophie's date, thinking that maybe he can roll it over in his mind and get used to the idea before getting home at the end of the week. "Hi, you," I said as I picked up my phone and saw Josh was calling.

"Hi, back," he said, "What's going on in Fort Dodge, Iowa these days? Anything?"

"As a matter of fact, LOTS! There is a swimming meet again tomorrow night and Sophie is swimming her usual butterfly and freestyle, along with the backstroke this time!"

"Wow, when did she start swimming that stroke?" Josh asked. I was actually kind of amazed that he realized the backstroke was not her usual stroke since he comments very little about her swimming.

"Just this week! She's a little nervous about it since she feels she doesn't have the turn down pat yet. The turn is backwards, since she will be on her back instead of her tummy, you know," I said.

"Right. What else is going on?"

"Bonding. I feel Sophie and I are doing a little bonding here lately."

"Really?" Josh said in disbelief. "I'm so glad you two girls are doing that! My two best girls in the whole world being friends—it's what I have wished for since the day you and I met!"

"Hold on, don't get too excited yet. I said 'a little' bonding. Don't go making us friends quite yet," I said laughing.

"Baby steps, okay, I get it," chuckled Josh. "Did anything in particular cause this 'little bonding' experience?"

"Well, there is a school dance coming up soon and a very nice, Christian boy from our church asked Sophie to go to the dance with him. Sophie asked me to help her with her hair and we went shopping and found the perfect dress…"

"Wait. What??" Josh interrupted. "What are you talking about? Sophie is only a freshman. She can't DATE."

Coffee, Anyone?

"Josh, the boy's mother is also from our church, and she is driving Sophie and Bradley to the dance. They are also picking up one of Sophie's good friends, Lindsey, to go with them to the dance, and I will be at the dance chaperoning."

"You what??" Josh said with unbelief.

"Sophie's date, Bradley's mother and I will be two of the adult chaperones at the school dance. The kids will not be out of our sight the entire evening."

By the brief silence that followed, I could tell Josh was contemplating, but then he said, "I don't want Sophie going to the dance, Amber. Discussion is over."

"Josh, this is some of what I want to talk to you about and when you get home, we will do just that—talk AND discuss. If I really am part of this family, I need to have some equal say in what goes on around here. I am not going to just carry out your groundings and orders like a prison guard when you are not even around and don't call me for days on end. You and I will discuss this like adults when you get home." Then I hung up.

Did I just DO that? My heart is beating so fast I can hardly breathe.

Amy Courter

I called Rachel and asked if Sophie could spend the night Friday with Lindsey. Now I had better be thinking about Josh's and my discussion come Friday night when he gets home from his trip. I am so out of my league on this one.

Coffee, Anyone?

Chapter 4
Sophie

"I can't believe I'm going to the daaannnce," I sang as I danced around my room in my beautiful homecoming dress. Lindsey brought her cute sandals to church last Sunday so I could try them on; they fit perfectly and look amazing with my stunning dress. I am so excited! Not quite so excited that Bradley's mom and Amber will be our chaperones that night, but if it means going, then I'm down with that. Bradley was so sweet when we were at youth group Sunday and he told Lindsey that she could be "our" date, too. He is the nicest human being in the world. I can't believe he likes ME!

I wonder what Amber will do with my hair for the dance. She does hers so amazingly. I hope she can make mine look something like hers. She seems so sophisticated. Maybe it really IS the Pilates that "keeps her grounded along with God" as she says. Maybe I really will try Pilates with her sometime. I know Amber is really trying to be a cool stepmom, and I am going to try very hard not to complain and be a brat. I am going to go find her and see if she has any jewelry that might go with my dress.

Amy Courter

"Amber!" I say loud enough to carry to all the rooms of our two-story Victorian house.

"In here," Amber replies from her bedroom down the hall.

I walk into her bedroom in my "new" sandals and dress and try to walk with confidence and poise. "You look gorgeous, honey! Absolutely beautiful."

I grin as I ask, "Should you put my hair up or leave it down for the dance, do you think? Also, do you have any jewelry that would go with my dress and not look too 'Mom-like'?"

As soon as I said "Mom-like" I knew I shouldn't have. Amber looked a little shell shocked when I said it, but I can't take it back now.

"Uh, well, how about this little heart locket, do you like it?" Amber asked.

"Maybe. What else do you have?"

"Let's see...I have a tiny stone necklace on a silver chain, another with little pearls on a gold chain..."

"Let me try them all on," I said, snatching the little pearled necklace from Amber's fingertips.

Coffee, Anyone?

"Oh, I like that one with the dress, do you?" Amber asked.

"How about this one?" I asked as I quickly traded one necklace for the other.

"That one works very well, too. You have a hard decision to make. How about earrings—do you have any that you want to wear of your own or do you want to look at some of mine?" Amber asked.

"Can I, really?" I asked.

"Absolutely! I need to go throw another load of laundry in downstairs, so take your time."

Chapter 5
Josh

I need to pick up the pace if I am going to make my flight out of Georgetown back to Des Moines tonight. Luckily, I travel light in case I need to run the last 100 yards or so.

Whew, made it with only a few minutes to spare. I hope my stomach behaves itself; I have had an upset stomach ever since my conversation with Amber Tuesday. I don't think she understands how threatening the world is out there; she just sees the good in people and not the evil that is running rampant. I do love that about Amber and her positive, upbeat attitude. It's part of what attracted her to me at the beginning of our relationship, as well as her smoking hot body, I smile to myself.

Coffee, Anyone?

Amber's outlook on life and all its goodness is starting to annoy me now, however. I feel she has no common sense sometimes and thinks all people are good people. "Give them a chance, Josh," Amber always says when I tell her about someone new at work that I don't trust. If I did that with every Tom, Dick, and Harry that I meet in my job, I would be dead by now. It's a dangerous place to be in this world currently and we need be aware of our surroundings, always thinking of the worst-case scenario so we are ready for whatever happens. That is my philosophy, anyway, although Amber calls me "the glass half empty guy".

I've tried to open up and let Amber into my world a bit; however, it's really difficult because of my role at the Federal Bureau of Investigation. I had to even tell a half-truth to Amber and Sophie as to where I work since we are not allowed to tell ANYONE the truth. It's very dangerous to have a family you love and want to protect from the evil world and now Amber is wanting to add to our family with a baby of her own. Not good. That would mean more loved ones to worry about and protect. It's not going to happen. I forbid it.

Amy Courter

Then there is Sophie who Amber is treating like a young adult and letting her go on dates and dances with boys, I thought, shaking my head. This is so much to deal with. Amber should NOT have told Sophie she could go to the dance without checking for my approval. I will need to make that very clear to her. Surely Amber is not right in thinking that Sophie should be able to go to the dance at 14 years old!

My former wife, Denise always told me that my negativity drove her crazy and it was the major reason she wanted to leave me at the end. Sighing, I think, I can't screw up this marriage, too. I need to at least give Amber a chance to explain, and I need to seriously think about what she is proposing and not go ape shit.

***

"Honey, I'm home!" I yell as I unlock the front door and take off my coat. "Anybody here?"
"Yes, I'm up here," I hear Amber say softly, from the bedroom area upstairs.

As I climb the steps and approach our bedroom loosening my tie and shedding my suitcoat, I stop dead in my tracks as I see naked Amber sprawled seductively across the bed with candles lit and rose petals scattered on the floor and bed.

Coffee, Anyone?

"Hello, handsome, thought you would never get home. Come on over here and give a girl a kiss, will you?" Amber drawled, as she handed me one long stemmed red rose.

"I can certainly do that," I stuttered, trying to think of something wittier to say, but coming up with zilch. My other head is thinking, though, that's for sure, as I look down at my trousers. She is so damn sexy. I can hardly wait to take Amber in my arms and make sweet love to her. I growl in my throat and do just that.

***

"Is Sophie in bed asleep?" I ask as we have pillow talk.

"No, Sophie is spending the night with her friend Lindsey and yes, Lindsey's mom, Rachel, is home. I checked," Amber said and continued, "I thought we needed a little time to ourselves to catch up on the last few weeks and also discuss some things."

"That was a good idea, Amber. You go first; what's on your mind?" I asked, hoping she isn't going to push the baby issue for at least a few more years.

"Josh, in order to make this marriage work, we need to be a team, do you agree?" Amber asked.

Amy Courter

"Well, sure," I said reluctantly, bracing myself for a trap.

"You are out of town sometimes for weeks and I need to have your trust that I can make some good decisions of my own," she went on to say, "I realize we should have discussed Sophie's date before I gave her the thumbs up, but you had not called for several days, and I was a little miffed."

"Amber, I told you…" I started.

Interrupting, Amber said, "Yes, I know you said you were busy on a case. Well, we are busy here at home, too, leading our lives or at least trying to. You have not yet met our friends at church and don't know them like Sophie and I do. Can you trust me that I am a good judge of character? Afterall, I knew you were a good man, right?" Amber smiled. "I know you leave for work Sunday evenings, and you aren't able to go with us to church, but I'm just asking for some trust here that I know some good people when I see them and get to know them. I love Sophie, Josh, and I would never deliberately put her in a harmful situation. I want the best for Sophie, but if we don't let her grow up in baby steps, trust me, she will rebel."

I tried to listen and stay calm, but finally said, "Amber, you do not know what boys are thinking and I do. They want ONE thing and that is to get into a girl's panties," I finally spat.

Coffee, Anyone?

"Really," Amber said, narrowing her eyes, "It seems to me you were able to behave yourself for quite some time before that happened when you were courting me."

"Well, it wasn't easy, and I thought about it ALL the time," I sheepishly admitted.

"Josh, the kids are 14. They are being driven to and from the dance by Bradley's mother, who is a lovely woman, and she and I will BOTH be at the dance watching over Sophie and Bradley. Can you trust that this is a safe situation, and no harm can come of this arrangement?" Amber pleaded.

I sighed, thinking this is like a chess move and I had to know the next move and the move after that before I answered anything. I carefully said, "Amber, can we agree that Sophie can only go to school-related functions for dates and no car dates until she is older?"

I could see Amber's mind calculating HER next move as she said, "Yes. That sounds very reasonable, Josh. I think Sophie will feel that is fair as well."

Well, that wasn't too awfully painful I thought until Amber kept talking.

Amy Courter

"Josh, when Sophie gets home in the morning, she has been dying to try on her homecoming dress for you. I want you to know that I did not have to remind her once about being decent with her choice. Sophie's dress covers her nicely and no cleavage is showing, not too much leg is showing, and her back is not bare. Believe me, there were dresses that had very little cloth to them, and she avoided even trying those on. Sophie has a good head on her shoulders, Josh, and I am really hoping that you will acknowledge that and give her a little more credit where credit is due. Do you think you can do that?"

"I suppose I can, but you will probably have to remind me," I said with a painful smile.

"I can do that," Amber said, as she flashed me her pearly whites.

"So, tell me more about this Bradley and what he is like," I said.

"Do you want to meet him? We could invite his family for supper one night if you would like," Amber answered.

"No, I would not like," Josh snorted. "Just tell me a bit about him. Is he a jock or into music, what?"

Coffee, Anyone?

"Bradley is on the tennis team, I know," Amber said, "And Sophie told me he has a huge heart. Bradley could see that Sophie's friend, Lindsey, felt a little left out after Bradley asked Sophie to the dance, so he invited Lindsey to go along with the two of them. They are like the Three Musketeers!"

Growing a teenaged girl is going to kill me, I thought, as I gave Sophie a tight-lipped smile. Baby steps…baby steps I kept repeating to myself.

"I promise to run things by you first concerning Sophie so we can parent together, if you will also promise to lighten up on the groundings and discuss those with me before barking out, 'You are grounded'. Let's try to really <u>listen</u> to Sophie. She's a good girl, Josh. You and Denise have done a wonderful job in raising her, and I am really tired of being the jailer and holding the hostage captive," Amber said seriously.

"I have a lot to think about and wrap my head around, Amber. I know I am too paranoid and negative at times, but a lot of it stems from my job and the people I deal with every day. I know this is going to be extremely hard for me, but I will seriously make an effort to be a more understanding parent and husband. I love you, Amber Jackson, and I love having you in my life. Are you "up" for Round Two, because I am," I said wiggling my eyebrows.

Amy Courter

Chapter 6
Amber

"Mags, you were SO RIGHT in your suggestion of taking Josh to bed BEFORE the parent-husband-changes discussion! It worked miraculously! And it was so much fun," I winked, as I finished hugging my co-worker, Maggie Monday morning.

"Well, any more advice will cost ya," Maggie said as she wrinkled up her cute little button nose and then added, "Kidding. I'm going to be counting on some good advice from you one of these days and know you will have it for me as well. That's what good friends do for each other!"

"Got that right, sista," I said as I was scrolling through my phone. "I want to show you this up-do I like and want to try on Sophie for the dance Saturday night. Can I practice it on you at lunch?"

"Sure, honey, I am here at your beck and call! Just name the time and place and I will be there! I promise to be the guinea pig of your stylish hair fantasies ANY time," Mags said.

Coffee, Anyone?

Mags is such a doll, I thought as I drove to pick up Sophie later that day. She never gets tired of combing out all that hairspray and product I use on her. She always tells me I missed one of my niches in being a hairdresser. No thanks, I shake my head, though it might be fun for a while. I much prefer the job I have in managing the hotel. I can use my hair skills as a hobby; it does come in rather handy sometimes. Maybe I will try the new up-do on Sophie tonight after supper to see if she likes it. If she doesn't like it, I do have another up-do in mind.

Sophie has another swim meet Wednesday night, and she will be swimming the backstroke again along with the butterfly and freestyle. I know she is a little nervous about it, although she has been working on that upside-down-turn for a couple weeks now and feels more confident about it. Her coach told me that she really appreciates Sophie and her willingness to try something new. Not all the swimmers will do that, she said. Sophie really likes to come in first and last week when she swam the backstroke, she came in second.

"Hi, Soph," I smile as Sophie jumps in my Prius. "How was your day?"

"Okay. I got a B on my algebra test. Better than I thought I would do. How about you? Did you have a good day?" Sophie looked over at me.

Amy Courter

My heart skipped a beat as Sophie's eyes met mine as she looked genuinely interested in hearing about my day.

"That's a great job, Sophie! Nothing wrong with a B at all! WAAAY better than I did in algebra, let me tell you! My day was okay, too. Mags let me practice an up-do on her at lunch today. Want me to try it out on you to see if you like it enough to wear it to the dance on Saturday?"

"YES! I have been dying to know how you are going to do my hair for Saturday!" Sophie exclaimed enthusiastically.

"Okay, meet you upstairs in about 10 minutes," I said as I pulled into the garage. "I want to toss some veggies into the microwave while we are working on your hair."

***

"I LOVE it!" crowed Sophie as I put the finishing touches on one last curl. "But do you think it will stay up there the whole night? I really don't like much hairspray, but I suppose it is necessary, right?"

Coffee, Anyone?

"Afraid so. I don't know how to make it stay put without the spray, honey. I will try not to use too much so that you feel like your hair might break in two or be crunchy if someone touches it, but it is really the best I can do. Unless you want to try just leaving it mostly down and just bringing the sides up?" I asked.

"Hmmm. Could we try just pulling the sides up sometime this week?" Sophie asked looking at herself in the mirror sideways and with her head tilted. "Although I really do like this up-do. I don't want to be a lot taller than Bradley, though."

I stifled a giggle as I was pretty sure Sophie was at least a head shorter than Bradley.

"You bet, let's plan to do that maybe tomorrow night. Do you want to leave your hair up while we eat to try to get used to the look or do you want me to take it down?"
"I'll leave it alone for now, but after supper, can I send a selfie to Lindsey to see if she likes it?" Sophie asked innocently.

Knowing Josh wouldn't like something that could be re-sent to others, I said, "As long as you send it to just Lindsey on snapchat where it disappears later, you should be fine. Deal?"

Amy Courter

"Yup!" Sophie said as she began to set the table. I got the rice and cheese ready to mix with our hot veggies as Sophie finished pouring us each a glass of skim milk.

"Would you like to say grace tonight or do you want me to?" I asked as we both sat down at the kitchen table. Sophie hesitated, but then said, "You can do it."

"Okay. Dear Heavenly Father, we are so very thankful this evening for your presence in our lives. We thank you for leading us to the perfect shop, the perfect dress, and the perfect boy for Sophie's first dance. We ask that you help keep us focused on you and your amazing grace each day. Thank you for this food before us and for all you do, in Jesus' name we pray. Amen."

Sophie looked up slowly and said, "Is it hard to pray? I mean, how do you know what to say to God? Does He get mad if you don't say the right thing or forget to thank him for something?"

"No, honey. God does not get mad at how you pray to Him. He doesn't care if you use the most 'enormous sophisticated, explanatory' words available. He just wants you to talk to Him from your heart. Tell Him what's on your mind. He wants to know every worry or concern you have so He can help you through it. He wants to have a relationship with you."

Coffee, Anyone?

Amber was silent for a moment and then said, "Cool," and began to eat.

Chapter 7
Sophie

"Amber, can Lindsey spend the night on Friday and then we can get ready for the dance together here on Saturday?" I asked as we were pulling out of the driveway.

"That sounds like fun," Amber said. "You can ask Lindsey today at school and I'll call Rachel to see if it is okay tonight. I'll also need to let Bradley's mom know to pick both you girls up here rather than at Lindsey's and here."

"That's okay, Amber, I will let Bradley know today and he can tell his mom," I said.

"Alrighty then!" Amber looked over and smiled at me.

***

Last night after supper Amber worked on my hair and just pulled the sides up, curling the rest and I looked amazing, if I don't say so myself, I thought grinning. Yeah, Amber isn't so bad. I am really trying hard to do everything she asks of me so she knows she can trust me and count on me.

Coffee, Anyone?

I was really bummed out after swimming the backstroke last week and only getting a second place for it last week. I wanted to quit swimming it until Amber started telling me how awesome I looked and how well I did, especially swimming the backstroke competitively for the first time ever. Coach wanted me to swim it again and I got another second, but I did place first in the other two categories, so two blues and a red aren't too bad, I guess. Maybe I will get better at the backstroke the more I do it. Regionals are coming up soon—YIKES.

***

"Oh, your dress is GORGEOUS, Lindsey! Did you meet Muriel at the chic shop I told you about?" I asked, after Rachel dropped off Lindsey's dress this morning.

"Yes, she is kind of 'gushy', isn't she?" Lindsey said with big eyes and a huge smile.

"Yeah, she likes to hug a lot and tell you how beautiful you are, but I kind of liked her," I shrugged.

"Me too," said Lindsey. "Glad Mom could pick the dress up last night in Des Moines so I could have the dress this morning. Hey, do you think your mom could do MY hair, too?" Lindsey asked hopefully.

Amy Courter

I didn't even cringe when Lindsey said "your mom"; in fact, I hardly noticed it, but felt I still needed to correct her. "How about if we go ask Amber. I bet she will!" I said enthusiastically.

Amber said, "Sure, Lindsey, I would love to do your hair! You have such a nice, thick head of hair! What are you thinking you want me to do with it?"

Lindsey said, "I think I will let Sophie go first and if I like hers, I will have you do mine like hers."
Amber said, "That works for me!"

I said, "Me too! We can be twins!"

***

After pictures with Bradley standing proudly between Lindsey and me, his mom took us to the dance. It was a bit awkward at first since none of us had ever been to a school dance before. For one thing, we saw that several guys and girls had flowers pinned to their dress or shirt. Ugh. I didn't even THINK about flowers! I guess this is a learning experience…another one! I should be VERY smart my senior year at this rate!

Coffee, Anyone?

I looked around the room and caught Amber's eyes while chaperoning. She didn't wave and make a spectacle of herself and embarrass me; she just smiled at me. She. Looked. So. Amazing. I don't know when she had time to do her OWN hair after doing ours and feeding us and helping us get ready, but she obviously doesn't need much time to look like that. I wish Dad could see her now. He is so lucky. I am so lucky, too, I thought as I smiled and turned away.

It was a fun night, and I will go to bed with a smile on my face, I thought as Bradley's mom drove us all home.

Several weeks after the dance, a sophomore girl, Chloe, came up to me at my locker and told me to thank "my mom" for her and I asked her why.

Chloe said, "I was stupid and drank before coming to the dance a few weeks ago and your mom saw me right away when I came into the school. She came at me like a hawk and whipped me off to the bathroom in a different corridor of the school that nobody was using and called my mom to come and get me. She waited with me for my mom to come and asked me what was going on."

Amy Courter

"I had barf running down the front of my dress and my mascara was all smeared and ugly. I was trying to impress the boy that I was with, and everything got out of control. I don't normally drink but James said he wanted me to relax, and the booze would help. It didn't help and it made me sick. I heard later that James had only asked me to the dance to win a bet with his friends. The bet was to get me drunk and embarrass me at the dance so all his friends could laugh and see he accomplished what he set out to do."

"Your mom listened without judging me and asked me if I would be going out with James again. When I said, "No!" she said, "That a girl! He doesn't deserve you.""

"She also walked me out to the car and asked my mom to not be too hard on me and that I would explain."

"If your mom had not grabbed me right away and taken me to a bathroom that other people were not using, the whole school would be gossiping. Right now, it just looks like James is a liar and never came through on his bet even though he was bragging he did. Anyway, I owe her my reputation and just wanted to thank her."

Coffee, Anyone?

Chloe turned around and left my locker with my mouth hanging open. How did Amber know how to handle that situation? Wow. She didn't say a word about this to me. I have renewed respect for Amber. She did good.

Amy Courter

Chapter 8
Josh

Amber sent me pictures of Bradley, Lindsey, and Sophie before they all left for the dance. Sophie is growing up before my very eyes. It makes me sad, I thought, but happy too. She is a beautiful young lady now. Denise would have been proud of Sophie, too. Too bad things ended the way they did with Denise. I know she didn't love me anymore and wanted to leave me. Our neighbor, Nellie, supposedly a good friend of Denise's, told me that Denise was having an affair and thought I should know about it. I wish I would have never known about the affair, I thought angrily.

Coffee, Anyone?

Chapter 9
Nikki

"How may I help you, sir?" I asked, as a 20-something handsome young man stepped up to my window at the Des Moines hotel.

"I need to talk to Amber Melone," the boy said.

"Amber does not work at this hotel any longer," I said, "Is there something that I can help you with?"

"No. Do you know where she is? I need to speak with her."

"May I ask what this is about, sir?" I asked.

The young man hesitated and said, "Amber Melone is my mom."

I realized my mouth was hanging open, so I closed it and said, "May I take your name and number and I will get hold of Amber and give her your information?"

"Okay," he said reluctantly.

Amy Courter

Ohmygosh, I think as I watch the young man walk out the door. Amber has a son!

"Amber? Do you have a few minutes to chat?" I asked her when I heard her voice on the phone.

"Let me call you back in five, Nikki. The front desk is CRAZY right now."

"Great, thanks," I said as I hung up.

When Amber called me back later and I told her about the young man, she was silent for the longest time. "Amber, you alright?"

"Yes, just thinking," Amber replied. "I was afraid this might happen someday."

"So, it's true?! You have a son?!" I asked incredulously. "You never mentioned him, EVER."

"Yeah, it was a very dark time in my life, about 19 years ago, before I knew you," Amber said slowly. "I did leave the adoption open so that he could come and find me if he ever chose to do that. I must have hoped he would do that one day, but now I am scared to death."

"Of what? Of Josh and what he will think?" I asked.

Coffee, Anyone?

"That, and the questions my son will ask me, like why did I give him up."

"Why did you give him up? If you want to tell me, that is," I asked curiously.

Amber sighed and said, "It was a long time ago, but I remember it like it was yesterday. I have thought about my son. Every. Single. Day. I was dating the quarterback in high school and thought he loved me. When I told him I was pregnant, he acted like it was all MY problem. He had a scholarship in football at the university and PLANS, he said. Didn't he think that I may have plans, too? I kept hoping I would miscarry, so I wouldn't have to make a decision and pretty soon it was too late to make any decision other than to have the baby. I was in no position to be a mom at 18 and my parents were not very supportive of me keeping the baby, so I gave him up for adoption hoping he would go to the perfect, loving family."

"I'm so sorry, Amber, that must have been a very lonely and confusing time for you," I said sadly.

"Yes, it was, but it is also when God became very real to me and I knew without a doubt that He loved me and had a plan for me, so some good came out of the situation, even though I felt like my heart had broken into a million pieces."

Amy Courter

"Ah, I always wondered at what point of your life you became a Christian," I said.

"It often happens when you are at rock bottom that you meet the Savior," Amber replied.

"Amen," I said. "Now what are you going to do?"

"Well, I am going to call him. You said his name is Jeremy, right?"

"Yes, that's what he told me."

"And after that, I need to let Josh know," Amber sighed.

"Good luck, my friend. Call me if you need some verbal courage," I said.

"Thanks, Nikki. Talk to you later."

Coffee, Anyone?

Chapter 10
Amber

I sat at my desk numb with disbelief, thinking and praying and thinking... I told Nikki I would call Jeremy first, but my heart is telling me that I need to talk to Josh first. That is what I will do this coming weekend when he is home. I have no idea how he is going to react to this news, I thought, sadly.

As I made my way through the week in a stumbling trance, even Sophie asked me at one point if I was okay. I told her I just had a lot of work stuff on my mind.

***

After we finished supper Friday night and Josh was helping me with the dishes, I said a quick prayer and told Josh about the phone call. Sophie was already on her phone with friends.

"You aren't going to call him back, are you?" Josh asked incredulously.

"Yes, I need to," I said quietly.

Amy Courter

"Well, how do you know he is actually your son and not some predator or someone wanting to rip you off. Fuck. Do you know anything about him, Amber?"

"I googled him and found out his birthday is the same day I had my baby. He grew up in Storm Lake, Iowa, not far from Laurens, my hometown. It's a start," I said.

"Well, I don't think you should call him. He has his family, and we have our family, and he could be dangerous. What does he even want?" Josh asked as he paced the kitchen.

"That's what I need to find out, Josh," I said seriously.

"Why am I just finding out about this? Why didn't you tell me earlier?" Josh asked as he narrowed his eyes. "Didn't you trust me?"

"I should have told you. I didn't think I would ever meet him and that's why I never told you about him. Hindsight is 20-20," I said sadly.

"Well, I don't want to have anything to do with this...this 'situation'," Josh sputtered as he spun around and headed to his office.

Josh will come around I kept whispering to myself as I did my chores on auto pilot. He will come around...

Coffee, Anyone?

But he didn't come around all weekend. He was moody and prickly and a real JERK. I wanted to discuss Jeremy further, but Josh was not giving an inch and left Sunday night without even giving me a kiss goodbye. It brought tears to my eyes.

***

"Amber, there's a call for you, line two," our receptionist buzzed me.

"This is Amber, how may I help you?" I asked.

"Amber, this is Roy, the private investigator you hired several weeks ago to look into your husband, Josh."

I had forgotten all about calling Roy and also about calling him OFF, but too late now. "Oh, Roy, so sorry for wasting your time. I don't need to have Josh investigated now. What do I owe you for your time and expenses?"

"Are you sure, Amber? I found some interesting information about Josh. I think you will want to take a look at it since you paid for it."

I had hired Roy, a friend and PI that I trusted from Des Moines when Josh didn't come home for three weeks in a row. I probably should have calmed down after our phone conversation when Josh told me he wasn't coming home. But now Roy had my curiosity piqued.

Amy Courter

"What did you find out, Roy?" I asked, bracing myself.

"I am e-mailing you some pictures to see if you know this guy. Josh is living with him, and they go out to dinner together all the time," Roy said.

"Thanks, Roy," I said as I thought over what Josh had told me about Georgetown and where he was staying. I thought for sure he said he had a company-provided condo in Georgetown. Why would some guy be living there with him?

What the heck! I thought as I flipped through the pictures on my cell phone. I couldn't believe this. Josh had his arm around this guy's shoulders as they walked out to the car! Josh is smiling at him over dinner. WHO IS THIS MAN?!

I hadn't prepared myself for the possibility of Josh cheating on me with a MAN, but could this be right?? Could Josh be bi-sexual? For Pete's sake, I need to call Roy back and find out more.

Could my life become any more confusing and conflicting right now? I don't think so. If I were a drinking woman, I would go get drunk right now, I thought. Instead, I said a quick prayer and asked God to please not let this be true. I'm so very miserable right now.

Coffee, Anyone?

"Roy, Amber here. Can you find out who this guy is, please, and WHY he is with Josh? I need to know and thanks for uncovering this for me. I appreciate it."

I didn't call Josh all week and Josh didn't call me. This is not good. I still haven't called Jeremy to find out what he wants (if anything). I feel like I am stuck with my feet nailed to the ground until Josh and I talk. Even when that happens, what could Josh possibly say that would make this picture innocent? I cannot imagine. I feel sick. I can't eat a thing and I haven't been sleeping well either. What if Josh IS bi-sexual and has a lover in Georgetown? What am I going to do about it? I love Josh and I love Sophie, but Josh can't have two lovers.

Chapter 11
Josh

It just burns my butt that Amber wasn't honest with me and didn't tell me about this kid she had 19 years ago. I mean, who keeps something like that a secret? She had to know it would come out eventually.

She lied to me. Wait. Maybe I didn't ask her if she had any kids. I guess, looking back, no, I didn't. I asked her if she had been MARRIED before and she said no. Still. She should have told me long ago. This is huge and could affect us. What if this kid hates his parents now and wants to live with us? What if he wants money to keep it quiet? What if he is on drugs? This is terrible, just terrible. I am going to get my people on this immediately to investigate this kid. I just hope to hell Amber hasn't called him back yet and welcomed him into OUR family with open arms. That would be just like her to do something like that.

As if I don't have enough on my mind, Sophie called me last night. She is worried about Amber and said Amber is so sad and not herself. She actually told me she really likes Amber and that I should "fix" things.

Coffee, Anyone?

I want to try that new BBQ place in town tonight; hopefully, Erin is up for it. Maybe a few hours unwinding with Erin will help me forget about Amber and all her shit.

Chapter 12
Amber

Roy sent me more pictures of this Asian guy that is living with Josh. Correction: Josh is living with the Asian guy; it's his condo! Roy found out his name, too. Josh has never mentioned an "Erin" so this can't be good. If he is a good friend, Josh would have, at some point, mentioned him at least. I guess I need to figure out my next step. Should I continue with the Private Investigator, or should I confront Josh, or should I just leave? No, I can't just leave. There is Sophie to think about and I should at least hear Josh out. I'm dreading his next weekend home because I'm afraid of what I will hear.

Josh hasn't called me all week so that tells me something. He really hangs on to his resentment and issues and has already decided I'm the unforgiveable one since I had a baby 19 years ago and failed to divulge that information to him. I'm thinking an affair is definitely worse since it is going on TODAY right under my nose, and with a MAN no less. This hurts me so much; I can hardly breathe today.

***

Coffee, Anyone?

Josh slides in beside me at the state swim meet Friday night. I put on my best fake smile and scoot over so he can sit comfortably. Great, now I have to figure this out THIS weekend. I was hoping for a little more time, but truth be told, I can't go on like this for much longer. I'm a HOT MESS.

"Go, Sophie!" we both yell as Sophie and the others line up in the water for the backstroke. As the gun goes off, I see Sophie make a huge surge backwards and take off like a pro. I'm so proud of that girl and how hard she works at accomplishing something new. "You GOT this, Sophie!" I yell as she continues her swim after a flawless flip and push at the side. It's going to be close I observe as the girl on Sophie's left also is swimming strong and staying right up there in the lead with Sophie. I couldn't tell who touched first. They are checking the touch pads and it was Sophie!!! I am so thrilled for her! Josh and I stand, clapping, and give each other a hug (for Sophie's sake). I can see Sophie walking back to her team's corner with a huge smile on her face as she pants heavily.

My first instinct is to show Josh the pictures on my phone of Erin and him; however, I want to make sure I can see his face and eyes when I do that. A person can tell a lot by looking into someone's eyes to find out if something is true or not. For now, we need to act normal, for Sophie's sake, and we will need to talk it out later.

"How was your trip?" I ask as we wait for Sophie to dry off and meet us after the swim meet.
"Fine," Josh replies. "Did you call that kid back yet?" he asks.

"No, I wanted to talk a little more with you before I do that," I replied. "In fact, we have a lot to discuss, you and I," I boldly said.

After supper and a board game called *Blank Slate* with Sophie, Josh, and me, Sophie disappeared to her room, leaving Josh and me alone. I was trying to decide the best way to ask Josh if he was having an affair, and decided to JUST DO IT.

"Josh, who is this man you are with?" I asked as I showed him the picture on my phone.

Josh squinted his eyes and looked at the picture getting angrier by the second. "Where did you get this?!" he shouted at me, nostrils flaring.

"Never mind that. I want to know who this person is and why you are living with him in Georgetown."

"Are you spying on me now, Amber?" Josh asked with a furrowed brow.

"Let's get back to my question. Who is this?" I calmly asked.

Coffee, Anyone?

I could tell Josh was still furious and didn't want to answer me, but finally, after a heavy sigh, he said, "His name is Erin Magee. He is a long-time friend of mine. We met at Boys State almost 25 years ago. We just hit it off and have been friends ever since. We were also roommates at University of Northern Iowa our freshman and sophomore years. The government recruited us both to work for them, so our paths crossed once again after Erin and I were assigned to the same case several years back."

"Why have you never mentioned Erin to me before if you were living with him and why ARE you living with him since you told me that you had a company-owned condo that you stayed at when in Georgetown?" I asked.

"Amber! Do you realize that poking into my work life could jeopardize my cases and even my life?! That was really a dumb thing to do! I can't believe you would take such a drastic measure! And I can't believe neither Erin or I noticed we were being watched and followed. That's our JOB to be aware of our surroundings!"

"I had to know what was going on, Josh. I went with my gut and my gut was telling me something wasn't right. No harm, no foul, right?" I questioned.

Amy Courter

"Dammit, woman! Don't you act like this was no big deal! You should have just asked me rather than to HIRE A PI, for fuck's sake!" yelled Josh.

"Okay, sorry, but I didn't feel I had a choice when I felt you were dodging my phone calls and then not coming home for three weeks...can you just answer my questions? Why aren't you living in your own condo in Georgetown like you told me?"

Josh sighed heavily and said, "It just seemed easier to share some expenses since we both had a condo and that way, we could catch up with each other's lives. I gave my condo up awhile back and moved into Erin's with him. Erin is not married and lives in his condo year around, so he had everything we needed. I didn't have to go out and buy a coffee maker or a toaster and all those household items."

I looked at Josh's eyes and could see no deceit, but I have been fooled before. "So, you and Erin go to work every day together and eat meals together, too?"

Coffee, Anyone?

"Yes, and since we are working the same cases 99% of the time, we are able to discuss our cases. It works out very well for both of us to have each other for a sounding board. Amber, you would not believe how hard it is not to tell you about my work, but I just can't. It would put you and Sophie in danger by telling you anything remotely close to my cases," Josh said with compassion in his eyes. "I hate it, but this is an outlet for me to unburden myself with Erin most evenings over dinner."

I'm still trying to wrap my brain around not knowing who this Erin character is and ask Josh, "Why didn't you invite him to our wedding? You said you had no close friends you wanted there. It would seem to me Erin would or should be pretty important to you if you spend that much time together."

I could see Josh's eyes dart left and then right as he thought about his response. "I told him about the wedding before I left for the three weeks I was gone. Guys are different than girls, Amber. Believe me, Erin didn't feel bad about not having to make that trip to Des Moines, Iowa, for the wedding."

"What IS *Boys State*, anyway? I have never heard of it," I asked.

Amy Courter

"Well, it was an honor to be chosen by the American Legion to attend the camp as a junior in high school. There are only two boys out of each state that are chosen. Erin was the other one from Iowa, although he lived in Emmetsburg, and I lived in Chariton. I did a little research on the program back in the day when I was chosen. Two guys started the hands-on program back in 1935, so it's been going on for the last 87 years. The high school juniors that are chosen become part of the function of government: local, county, and state. Because we were chosen for this honor, Erin and I both feel that is why we were recruited later after graduating college. We'd had a good taste of what the government is all about after our week at camp. The American Legion even PAID for most of our education!"

"How did you get chosen to be part of this group in the first place?" I was curious.

"I didn't know I was going to receive this honor but later learned that the school actually recommends a list of eligible candidates to the local Legion. Then the Legion chooses from there, interviewing if necessary. I don't remember being interviewed, though, so maybe my school didn't recommend anyone else."

Coffee, Anyone?

"My parents always told me that doing free stuff in my community gets a person noticed and they signed me up for lots of it. I'm glad they did; it really paid off in a big way. My folks didn't have a lot of money and I probably would have had to take out a student loan in order to go to college if *Boys State* hadn't paid most of my way. I was also able to get work on campus while going to college that helped with my room and board while there. My last two years at University of Northern Iowa, I was an RA, so I suppose that showed 'leadership' as well."

"You know, I learned more in one week at *Boys State* camp than I did in my high school civics class. We had hands on experience at camp! *Boys State* also showed me opportunities to get scholarships and even earn some college credit while still in high school."

"Erin and I actually volunteered in the summers as counselors at Camp Dodge in Johnston where we went to *Boys State*. I suppose that helped both of us, too, in being recruited by the government later after college," Josh said thoughtfully.

"Again, sorry. I guess I let my imagination run away and thought you might be having an affair. I hired a PI I knew from my Des Moines days to see if my suspicions were warranted."

Amy Courter

"Amber, seriously?" Josh asked incredulously. "You really and truly thought I would be having an affair and with a GUY? You know how beautiful you are, right? Why would I want or need anyone else?" Josh asked while caressing my cheek fondly.

"Well, sometimes you are very hard to read, Joshua Alan Jackson!" I brazenly stated.

"Don't think so hard, Amber Jackson. And call your watchdog off me! I'm mad that neither Erin or I realized we were being followed and watched. We should have FELT it. Dang. Losing my touch," Josh muttered.

"Yeah, okay, but Josh, you were chastising ME for keeping a secret from you and look at this big secret you kept from me! I was seriously thinking of leaving you if you were having an affair! Let's try to be more open and honest with each other going forward. Do you think we can do that?" I asked.

"I will absolutely try, Amber, but like I said, there are so many things I just cannot be transparent about. You will just have to trust me."

Coffee, Anyone?

"That's a two-way street, Josh. You need to trust ME as well. I need to call Jeremy, the baby boy I had 19 years ago, and find out why he tracked me down. Maybe he just wants to meet me and wants nothing from me. I promise to share the conversation with you after I call him," I pleaded.

Sighing, Josh said, "I suppose. I just don't like it. It doesn't feel right after all this time that he is looking you up."

"That may have been his parents' decision, not Jeremy's. He may have had to wait until he turned 18 to open the adoption record and get my name, so don't go all crazy on me. Tell you what, you tell me how you think this conversation should go with Jeremy," I said.

"He will probably want to meet you for coffee or lunch or something. Just DO NOT invite him here," Josh said.

"Yes, that is what I am thinking as well. I would also like to meet Jeremy. I have wondered about him for so long; does he have my blue eyes and blonde hair, and does he have any of my silly tendencies or habits? Are his teeth straight or does he have this one tooth that bends in a little like mine? This is a dream come true for me. I just didn't realize it until now," I said. "Do you want to come with me to meet him?"

Amy Courter

"No, I think it best if you met him by yourself. It would be less awkward if I were not there, but if you set it up for this weekend, maybe I could be lurking in a nearby booth, just in case, you know," Josh countered.

"I think I will call him now. It's only 10PM; he probably isn't in bed yet."

"Go for it, Amber, I'm going to go take a shower; see you upstairs in a bit?"

"Yes, now wish me luck, my heart is pounding out of my chest," I said.

"Here, let me see," as Josh put his hand on my chest or rather my breast. "Yes, you certainly are a scared little rabbit, aren't you?" he grinned his sexy smile.

"Go away now, you horn-dog!" I said as I gave him a push toward the stairs.

Okay. Breathe. In. Out. I can do this. "Jeremy?" I asked when the phone was answered.

"Yeah?" the voice said.

"This is Amber Jackson, I mean Amber Melone."
I decided to let Jeremy begin the conversation since I didn't know how to do it myself.

Coffee, Anyone?

Jeremy cleared his throat and said, "Yeah, um. I told your assistant that I wanted to talk to you…um. I'm your son you gave up for adoption 19 years ago. I…ah wondered…um…do you want to meet for coffee or something? I mean, if you aren't busy or..um…something."

"I would like that, Jeremy. Would tomorrow work for you or are YOU busy?" I asked.

"Umm…no…I mean…ah..yes, I can meet you tomorrow. I can come to Fort Dodge. Where do you want, you know, to meet?" Jeremy stammered.

"There's a Perkins at the east edge of town, would that work for you? About 11AM?"

"Umm, sure. That works. See you then." Click.

"Jeremy?" I guess he hung up. Well, I guess that went as well as it could go, I thought as I climbed the stairs for bed.

***

Amy Courter

That was the longest night of my life. I don't think I slept at all. I am so anxious I can hardly see straight. Josh and I have it figured out and he is going to be in the booth behind me with his back to me so he can hear our conversation. We plan to get there well before 11AM so we can pick our booths and order a carafe of coffee.

I forgot to tell Jeremy what I looked like! Will he know me when he walks in? I think I will know him, although his social media page didn't have a lot of pics of him that I could see. Hopefully, he will know what I look like. Maybe when we make eye contact, we will just know?

"Uh...Amber?" asked a long-haired blonde boy, about 5 ft 10 in tall.

"Yes, that's me!" I smiled hugely to cover for my nervousness. "Have a seat, Jeremy. Did you have far to drive? Where do you live?" Oh man, I talk like an auctioneer when I am nervous, so fast and one question after another after another. S-L-O-W down, Amber, I said to myself. Take a deep breath and let him speak.

"Not far," he said. "I go to school at Iowa State. I'm a freshman there," Jeremy said, while looking as nervous as I felt.

"Oh, what are you studying, Jeremy?" I asked.

Coffee, Anyone?

"I want to bet a vet so I have a ways to go yet. Just getting started," Jeremy responded.

Our waitress brought another cup to our table. I asked Jeremy if I could fill it and he nodded yes.

"That's a great goal! What helped you decide you wanted to be a veterinarian?" I asked genuinely interested.

"My dad is a vet so I guess I am following in his footsteps. I just like being around animals and helping them," Jeremy said, relaxing a little now.

"That's the college I went to as well, Jeremy, back in my day, you know. I majored in Hotel Management," I offered.

"Yeah, I found out some information about you that led me to the Des Moines hotel and after that it was a dead end," Jeremy said.

"I just got married a few months ago, so I suppose that is why," I said. "When did your parents tell you that you were adopted?" I ventured.

Amy Courter

"I was about seven or eight I think," Jeremy answered. "I was actually kind of shocked. I don't know what the perfect age is to find out you are adopted, but I really thought I should have been told a bit earlier."

I nodded in agreement and then asked, bracing myself, "Did you get your adoption opened to find my name or how did you know I was your birth mother?"

"Yeah, I went to the courthouse and got the information. My dad helped me. Since you requested that the adoption be an "open" adoption on your end, that helped a lot, so I didn't have to jump through a bunch of legal hoops. So, thank you for that. My parents made me wait until I was 18, though."

"Can you tell me about your parents, Jeremy?" I asked.

"Yeah, I guess. My mom is a third-grade teacher in Alta. It's not very far from Storm Lake in case you didn't know that. My dad is a veterinarian in Storm Lake. I am hoping I can get through vet school before he retires so we can work together at his clinic," Jeremy answered honestly.

Coffee, Anyone?

"I've wondered about you for so many years, Jeremy, and hoped and prayed you landed in a home with loving parents. I just couldn't give you that at 18 years old. It sounds like your parents are good people and you must admire your dad to want to follow in his footsteps?" I questioned.

"Yeah. I have good parents. They are paying for my college and have been good to me, so I guess you got your wish. What about you? What happened to you after you gave me up for adoption?" Jeremy looked at me carefully and said, "That is if you want to tell me about it."

"Sure, that's fine. I was able to go to Iowa State as well on a partial scholarship, after taking a semester off after high school to have you. I needed to work while attending college, so I found a job at a hotel near the ISU campus, working my way up to Assistant to the Assistant Manager of the hotel by the time I graduated with my degree. That's where I fell in love with the hotel business and decided to major in hotel management. I started out in Webster City at a hotel there for a few years, jumping around to different towns and hotels for several years until I landed the management job in Des Moines at *Visitors Matter*. I really loved the homey atmosphere and ended up staying there for about 10 years."

Amy Courter

"What made you leave Des Moines then?" asked Jeremy.

I held up my left hand and ring finger. "Marriage," I said simply. "I met my husband at our hotel in Des Moines. He used to stay with us every couple of weeks on a Sunday night to catch an early flight out on Monday morning."

"Oh, right. You told me you got married a few months ago," Jeremy nodded. "Where did you go from there? Another hotel in Fort Dodge?"

"Yes, I was able to transfer from the Des Moines *Visitors Matter* hotel to the Fort Dodge *Visitors Matter* hotel," I offered. I could hear Josh clear his throat behind me since he was sitting in the booth directly in back of me. I am guessing he doesn't want me to get too personal and offer too much information about myself or HIM. But, screw Josh, I may never get this opportunity again with Jeremy and I want to be open with him.

"Do you have any other kids?" Jeremy asked quietly.

"Yes, I have a 14-year-old step-daughter, named Sophie," I proudly said as I could feel Josh squirming around in his booth.

"Oh, wow!" exclaimed Jeremy.

Coffee, Anyone?

I laughed as I said, "Yes, raising a teen is a brand-new territory for me, that's for sure, but it's fun and Sophie is a great girl."

"And your husband? What does he do?" Jeremy asked.

I heard Josh cough before I said, "Josh works for the government."

"Ahh. I see. Umm. Do you know who my biological dad is…errr…his name was not on the original birth certificate."

"Yes, I know for sure who your dad is, Jeremy. He didn't want his name on the birth certificate, so I left it off. I'm sorry."

"That's okay. I know it was a long time ago and you guys were young. I was just wondering, you know. Can you tell me anything about him? Do I look like him?" Jeremy asked with hope in his voice.

"Your dad was about your height, but your coloring is more like mine. He was also a very good athlete in high school. Did you play sports in high school, Jeremy?" I asked.

Amy Courter

"Yeah, I was quarterback at my high school in Storm Lake. I played basketball, too. I was pretty fast, but too short to do much damage, you know," Jeremy said with a smile.

"You do take after your dad with your sports background," I said, "I was a cheerleader, so I could do cartwheels and backflips, but that is about it, although did you know that many schools are calling cheerleading a sport now?" I asked with a twinkle in my eye.

"Ha, no, I didn't know that, but it <u>should</u> be called a sport, really. I mean, it's more physical than golf and they call THAT a sport," Josh said earnestly.

"Right?" I nodded smiling.

"Um...I should be going. I have to get to work soon and still need to drive back to Ames. Uh...would you ever want to do this again with me?"

"I would absolutely like to do this again with you, Jeremy," I said as I smiled. "You have my cell number since I called you back."

"Okay, thanks, um. Amber? Is that what you want me to call you?"

"Sure, Amber is fine, Jeremy. I look forward to our next visit. Be well and drive safely!"

Coffee, Anyone?

"Yeah, I will. Thanks. And thanks for the coffee, too," Josh said as he slid out of the booth and walked to the door.

I sipped my cold coffee and watched Jeremy as he walked out the door and got into his car. Josh slipped into my booth across from me.

"Did you have to give him our names, for fuck's sake?" Josh barked at me.

Ignoring his outburst, I calmly said, "I think Jeremy is a very nice young man, how about you, Josh?"

Sighing loudly, he sputtered, "We still don't know what he <u>wants</u>, Amber. He never said what it is that he wants from you."

"Yes, he definitely did, Josh. Jeremy wants to have a relationship with me. He wants to know who I am, and he wants me to know who he is. And I want the very same thing," I said smiling. "Give him a chance, Josh."

Chapter 13
Sophie

Something is going on with Amber. I don't know what, but I think it is my dad's fault. I can tell something is bothering her BIG time, but when I asked her, she just said it was work stuff. Yeah, I'm not buying it. I even called Dad and told him I liked Amber and told him to FIX whatever is wrong. Like he listens to me ever, though. This morning Dad and Amber went out for coffee. Whatever it was they talked about, Amber sure seems happier--Dad, not so much. Amber seems to handle Dad much better than Mom ever did. Amber stands her ground and doesn't seem scared of Dad like Mom was. Maybe it's because Amber married later in life or something.

Tonight, after supper I saw a text on Amber's phone when I was walking by the den from a Jeremy that said, "It was my pleasure and nice meeting you, too." Below that Amber had texted, "It was very nice meeting you today, Jeremy. Thanks for reaching out!" I wonder what that is all about.

Coffee, Anyone?

Chapter 14
Josh

What a weekend, I thought, as I drove to the Des Moines airport for my trip back to Georgetown. I still cannot BELIEVE that Amber called a PI to investigate me! Who even DOES that?! I suppose I have given her reason to be suspicious when I try to look at it from her viewpoint. I probably should have told her about Erin. I just didn't want to complicate the issue. Amber wouldn't understand how important Erin is in my life, so I just avoided bringing it up. It seems like Erin has been in my life forever and is part of me. We have experienced so much together. He is my confidante, and I don't know what I would do without him.

She bloody hell better have called her PI off us, though, I thought shaking my head. I have to admit, Amber has moxie! Damn, for sure. It kind of turns me on, ha! I will definitely have to keep that in mind in the future, I thought to myself.

Amy Courter

I'm still thinking about her news about having a baby and giving it up back 19 years ago. And I'm still bothered about Amber hiding this from me. She should have divulged that information as soon as we were serious. Except, in all fairness, we weren't serious very long before we got married, I think with a grin. I just had to make sure I locked her down before someone else did and when she wouldn't move in with me without getting married, I knew I needed to put a ring on that girl's finger! She is kind of a pistol, though, I am finding out.

Denise was very compliant, and I rarely had trouble with her following requests, although she did say they were not "requests", they were "orders" from me. The last year with Denise was not a fun one. We fought most every weekend I was home, so I tried not to come home very often to avoid the whole ordeal. Denise just wasn't listening to me and wouldn't do what I told her to do. I had to involve our next-door neighbor, Nellie, with a little favor once or twice.

Coffee, Anyone?

I really am trying to be more receptive with Amber. It's this damn temper of mine. It gets me into so much trouble. Usually when I blow, that helps ME, but if my wife is the "blowee" that's not good. Amber keeps telling me that God could help me with my temper if I would ask Him. Yeah, that's not going to happen. I pretended to listen to Amber's spewing about God and what He has done for her and for everyone, sacrificing his only Son to die on a cross for us so that we can ALL be forgiven and live eternally with Him, blah, blah, blah, and I even told her I was a Christian because she told me she was a Christian. I thought it can't be too hard to fake, right? After I told her I was a Christian, she said, "Good, because I would never marry someone that isn't a Christian." It was a good thing I came up with that little fib! I needed it to get the girl!

Sigh, I'm realizing that I never "have to blow" when I'm in Georgetown with Erin; it's only when I get home to Amber that I have trouble with my temper. There are always stressful situations at home in Fort Dodge, plus I always have to watch what I say while in Fort Dodge; it's exhausting.

Chapter 16
Amber

"Sophie! You want to do some yoga/Pilates with me downstairs?" I called at the bottom of the staircase.

"Yeah, just a minute, though. I need to finish drying my hair, so it doesn't dry weird before we go to church tonight," Sophie yelled back.

"Okay, I will get the Roku set up," I said happily.

Thinking over the weekend, I am glad Josh and I had our talk. We have a lot of issues to work through. I really wish I hadn't jumped so fast into marriage. I'm trying not to judge him, but I feel like most of the issues are HIS.

"Amber?" Sophie asked, after 45 minutes of exercising to our yoga/Pilates leader online, we started with our cool down. "I was just wondering…did you have bullies in your school in Laurens when you were in high school?"

Coffee, Anyone?

Wondering where this was coming from, I said carefully, "I'm sure we did, Sophie. I didn't DO any bullying and was not the recipient of being bullied, but I do remember a few people that went out of their way to make someone else not feel welcome for even "talking" to us."

"Like how?" Sophie asked.

"Well, I remember one of my friends actually turned her back on a girl while we were standing in kind of a semi-circle before school started, closing the girl OUT of the circle and rolling her eyes when the girl kept talking. I thought it was kind of mean, but I didn't call her out on it. I should have, I realize, now, and probably would now adays but back then, I suppose I was just happy to be part of the in crowd," I said. "Any particular reason you are asking?"

"Yeah. My friend Lindsey is getting bullied at school by my 'old' friend, Beth. Lindsey has been nothing but kind to Beth, so Beth has no reason to be so mean to Lindsey. I don't know what her problem is."

"I don't know if you have ever told me about your 'old' friend, Beth. Who is she? And why is she an 'old' friend?" I asked.

Amy Courter

"Beth and I were friends in grade school and part of junior high. And then after my mom died, I told Beth a secret that had just been killing me to keep it to myself. I thought Beth would keep it to herself, but she told the whole school! I just couldn't forgive her for doing that to me. I would have never done that to her if she had confided in me about something she wanted to keep secret."

"Oh, I see," I said. "Do you think Beth's bullying to Lindsey could be because she misses you and your friendship and is jealous of you and Lindsey being friends?"

"I guess I hadn't thought about that being the reason," Sophie said sadly. "If it's my fault, I should try to fix this then, right?"

"Oh, I didn't mean it's your fault, honey, I just was trying to figure out why Beth would want to hurt Lindsey," I said quickly. "Have you or Lindsey ever asked Beth why she was being mean to Lindsey?"

"No. We just try to ignore her," Sophie said.

"Sometimes confrontation is the only thing that works with some people," I said. "Anyway, I would give her a chance to try to explain. Do you think she is seeking your forgiveness about what she did to you? I know it seems like a roundabout way, but just a thought."

Coffee, Anyone?

Sophie hesitated and then said, "I guess I will tell you what she did to me, so you have the whole picture. Right after my mom's death, I was so sad and confused. The police had taken Dad to the police station to question him. I started thinking that maybe my dad killed my mom. Dad wasn't sad like I was and didn't even cry about it. I felt like my whole world just blew up in my face and my dad was acting like it was no big deal. So, I told Beth that I was afraid that my dad killed my mom, she hugged me and told me she loved me, and I felt so much better after telling her my secret and getting it off my chest. When I went back to school about three weeks later, I found out that Beth told the whole school that I thought my dad killed my mom."

I swallowed and blinked fast to keep my tears in check and said, "Oh Sophie, that must have been devastating for you."

"Yeah, I have had better days for sure," Sophie said while shaking her head. "I talked to Dad about the cause of Mom's death later and he said it was from her severe peanut allergy and that it could have occurred a lot of different ways and that we will probably never know exactly what happened."

Amy Courter

"Oh, honey," I sadly said. "You know boys are a lot different than girls in the way they show their emotions. Your dad may have felt he had to be the tough, strong one for you. I'm sure your mom's death really rocked his world as well."

"I guess. It sure didn't look like he was very sad to me, though. I never did tell Beth that I changed my mind and don't think my dad killed my mom. I never talked to her after that," Sophie admitted.

"How did you know Beth told the whole school," I asked.

"The class big-mouth, Jody, told me at my locker that Beth told everyone that I thought my dad killed my mom," I replied.

"Can you think back and be sure that is exactly what Jody said? Maybe you just jumped to the conclusion that Beth told your secret? Could that be a possibility, Sophie?" I asked.

Sophie sat awhile thinking this over and finally said, "I need to talk to Beth and ask her point blank if she told the school about my secret."

I smiled and said, "I think that is a very good place to start, honey."

Coffee, Anyone?

Chapter 16
Nosie Nellie
(as Sophie likes to call her)

It's been almost 14 months now since Denise's death and Josh has not called me since he married Amber. After Denise died, Josh asked me to move into his house to take care of Sophie when he was traveling and I did that for almost a full year before he met Amber and married her, I thought angrily. I was certain he wanted us to be together as a family and then I find out that he asked Amber to marry him and told me that I could move back into my own home again. I could hardly contain my anger with his deception.

I put up with that brat Sophie for almost a year while she was mouthy and mean to me every day, but I did it for Josh. I knew I had to get along with Sophie to make it work with Josh, so I did what I had to do. And you bet I told Josh every single unkind thing that Sophie said to me, the little unpleasant child.

I practically gave up a whole year of my life by taking on this colossal endeavor of rearing this defiant daughter of his. I kept thinking, though, that it will all be worth it in the end.

Amy Courter

In the beginning when I got together with Denise, we had a real friendship going. I miss Denise. I wish she didn't have to die. We laughed and talked and shared recipes. Denise even invited me over for meals with her and Sophie now and then. I felt she was a good friend. But when she confided in me one day that she was having an affair with her boss, my feelings toward Denise changed. I just couldn't understand or condone that she was fooling around on Josh. Josh is a decent, loving person and did not deserve that. He worked so hard for his family and then she does the unforgiveable to him. What kind of decent person cheats on a good man like that?

After Josh told me he was getting married to Amber, I called him to talk about how he hurt my feelings and I thought he and I would marry. Josh actually laughed and told me that I was delusional and that he had NEVER mentioned marriage to me nor even hinted at it. While that may be, he certainly gave me lots of reasons I thought we would be together as a family. I put my life on the line for him and took a huge risk, but does Josh appreciate it? No, he tosses me aside like a rag doll. Well, I won't let him get away with it.

Coffee, Anyone?

Chapter 17
Amber

I looked at my phone after texting Jeremy. I could tell he was texting back. I had asked him how his big test went in World History. We've been texting back and forth at least a couple times of week since we first met. I enjoy this kid so much and would love to meet his parents sometime. They have done a fantastic job in raising Jeremy. What a nice young man he turned out to be.

He texted back, "Fine. I think I did pretty well on it. I think I finally have figured out what information the professor likes to include on tests—ha!" Then a thumbs up from me. I love this easy, friendly relationship Jeremy and I have going.

Chapter 18
Sophie

"Amber!" I exclaimed as she pulled up to get me from school. "I'm so glad you encouraged me to talk to Beth! She said she did NOT tell the school my secret and she kept trying to call me, but I wouldn't take her calls. She said she knew I would think that she told everyone. The only thing we could come up with is that Jody—remember the school gossip--has a police scanner because her dad is a cop. She probably heard they were taking Dad in for questioning. When I think back at what Jody said exactly to me at my locker, I don't remember her saying anything about Beth. I just assumed that Beth was the guilty culprit since I had told her my painful secret. I'm so glad that is cleared up! Thank you, Amber!"

"Wow! I am happy for you both and that you were able to work through the situation to restore your friendship," Amber said with a smile.

"Me too! Could I invite both Lindsey and Beth to spend the night Saturday. Pretty please?" I begged.

"Sure, that sounds fine, honey," Amber answered. "Your dad won't be home this weekend so that will be fun! Do you want me to call their moms and let them know I will be here?"

Coffee, Anyone?

"I guess if you want to," I said. "I don't think you really need to, but if you think you should, go for it."

"I always appreciate it when a parent calls me to let me know they are going to be home. It's a little awkward to call when the shoe is on the other foot, so I'm going to make it less awkward by giving each of the moms a call," Amber nodded.

"Okay, knock yourself out!" I yelled as I ran upstairs to finish my algebra for tomorrow.

I heard Amber yell back, "Dinner in 10 minutes!"

While we were eating, I said, "Amber, who is Jeremy?"

I thought Amber was going to choke on her food as she coughed, her face turning red. Finally, she took a swig of water and her eyes quit watering.

"Um. Why do you ask?" Amber finally was able to speak.

"I didn't mean to be a snoop or anything, but I was walking by the den and saw a text on your phone to Jeremy about meeting him and driving safe. You don't have to tell me if you don't want," I said as I looked down at my food.

Amy Courter

"No, it's okay, Sophie. I'll answer you," Amber began. "Jeremy is my biological son who I met for the first time last Saturday. He is a freshman at Iowa State University majoring in Veterinary Medicine. I had a baby when I was 18 and gave him up for adoption. That baby was Jeremy."

"Oh, I didn't know that," I stammered. "How did he know where to find you or that you were his biological mom?"

"There are different types of adoption you can choose and even the different options have several options within the options," Amber said. "The type I chose was called an 'open adoption' where I left my name so if Jeremy wanted to ever find me, he easily could. It must be a two-way street, so if his parents or he did not want me to find him or them, they would have a 'closed adoption' on their end and then nothing could happen on either end without jumping through a bunch of legal hoops. Jeremy's parents left their end closed until Jeremy turned 18 and then they opened their end and found that my end was open as well. Jeremy's dad helped him locate me."

"Were you surprised he called you?" I asked.

"I was, yes. But I also had expected it for a long time. Does that make sense?" Amber laughed.

Coffee, Anyone?

"Yeah, I think I understand. If he didn't call you then you could just forget about him and go on with your life, but if he DID call you, then you have to meet him and get to know him and stuff, right?" I asked.

Amber smiled and said, "Something like that. Anyway, Jeremy is a wonderful person, and I am looking forward to our next visit. Maybe you would like to meet him as well sometime?"

"Sure, I would like that!" I blinked over big eyes.

"Well, I will work on arranging that someday in the future. Right now, Jeremy and I are just getting to know each other. It sounds like he had very nice parents. His dad is a veterinarian and Jeremy wants to go into practice with him when he gets done with school. His mom is a third-grade teacher in Alta, Iowa," Amber told me.

"So, they couldn't have any kids of their own, is that why they ended up with your kid?" I asked.

"I don't know the particulars. That might be true and most likely is the reason, but I am so thankful that Jeremy ended up with a loving family. I prayed about that every day," Amber said.

"You really did that?" I asked. "Even when it was all over and he was adopted?"

"Oh, yes, I did. Every. Single. Day. I never forgot about him. Every year on his birthday, I would say to myself, 'My son is six today' or whatever age he was that year. Giving up a part of yourself is a big deal and I struggled a long time over it. It was part of what drew me close to God at that time," Amber said as she searched my eyes.

"I get that," I said. "Because God cares about everything and wants you to not worry about anything. Lindsey would know where that is in the Bible, but I don't," I said.

"Speaking of that," Amber said as she got up out of her chair, "I ordered you something the other day through Amazon."

"What is it?" I asked.

"Open it and find out!" Amber smiled.

Tearing open the package, I exclaimed, "A Bible! For me? I don't have to borrow yours anymore?"

"That's right, Sophie, this one is all yours," Amber said and continued. "You can highlight in it or underscore a passage you want to remember or make notes in it. It's yours to do what you want with it."

Coffee, Anyone?

"Thank you so much, Amber! I really appreciate this! I'm going to go call Lindsey and tell her I have my very own Bible now!" I yelled as I took off on a run up the stairs.

I called Lindsey as soon as I got to my room and shut the door. "Hey, Lins! Are you done eating yet? I should have looked at the clock and forgot."

"Yup, just finished. What's up?" Lindsey asked.

"Well, Amber just said I can invite you for a sleepover Saturday and get this: I talked to Beth after algebra class today and asked her if she told the school that my dad killed my mom and she said she didn't and she would never do that to me. She kept trying to call me, but I wouldn't answer her calls. So, she got mean to you because she missed me. Do you think you can forgive her?"

"I suppose I have to like God says," answered Lindsey.

Amy Courter

"I was hoping you would say that, because I am going to invite Beth to come over and spend the night with us, too! Hey, do you think we could see if she wants to start coming to church with us on Sunday nights?" I asked without waiting for an answer and said, "Oh, guess what else? Amber had a baby a long time ago named Jeremy and he goes to ISU studying to be a veterinarian! And you know what else? Amber gave me my very own Bible! I can write in it if I want to, like you do, to remember stuff! I'm so excited!"

Lindsey started laughing and said, "I can see that! Let me go ask my mom if I can come Saturday. Hang on."

Coffee, Anyone?

Chapter 19
Amber

I sat down with a good book I have been trying to finish now for a couple of weeks. I was hearing the three girls upstairs with their giggles and fun and it made me smile. I remember those days. So carefree and happy.

"Hey, Amber," Sophie yelled coming down the stairs, "Can we make a snack in the kitchen? We will clean up after ourselves."

"Sure, honey! I'll be just around the corner in case you need me," I said.

Amber yelled upstairs, "Come on down, Lindsey and Beth!"

As the girls trampled down the stairs and headed for the kitchen together, I'm a little worried. I don't want anyone to go home without a finger or two if they plan to use the mixer. I guess there is a time when you just have to trust, though, and I have shown Sophie how to be careful when we have made cookies together. She knows what the mixer can do if you get too close to the blades.

Amy Courter

Sounds like they are making brownies from a box, and you don't have to get the mixer out for that, so whew! I will be able to send the girls home with all their digits in place now, I think with a smile.

When I was upstairs earlier, collecting dirty laundry to wash, I heard Beth apologize to Lindsey telling her she was sorry for being so mean to her. I was very relieved to hear that she chose to ask for forgiveness rather than to just have Sophie ask Lindsey. It means a lot more when the person asking for forgiveness is the person that NEEDS forgiveness.

I also heard Beth tell Sophie that "Amber is so cool! You are soooo lucky!" I heard Sophie answer back, "Yes, she is very cool!" I thought with a smile. I feel pretty darn lucky, too. It's terrifying being a stepmom and trying to discipline but wanting a good relationship, too. Those first few months were not fun AT ALL. But we got through it, and I think we are going to be okay, I thought happily.

Oh, I hear all three girls trampling down the stairs again with their hairbrushes, hairspray and a basket full of clippies.

"Amber, would you do something fun with our hair?" Sophie asked. "We each have our own brush."

Coffee, Anyone?

"Sure," I said as I put down my book. "Who wants a French braid?" I heard three, "I Dos!" "How about if I teach you how to do a French braid and you can practice on each other?"

"Yes!" Lindsey said excitedly. "You do Sophie's, and I will do Beth's hair while watching you."

"Okay. The first thing we will need is a little squirt bottle with water. Oh, I see you even brought me one of those! Good thinking, Sophie!" I commented. "Just spray the water lightly so the hairs will stick together but not too much that the hair is sopping wet."

"Oh, this is going to be fun!" exclaimed Lindsey, as she started gathering pieces of Beth's hair at the crown of her head.

"Take your time and gently just keep adding more hair pieces each time. Try to keep the braid going in the same direction so you have a nice straight braid at the end," I said.

Frowning, Lindsey said, "Oh, mine doesn't look as good as yours, Amber."

"Well, I have done this for a while. Practice makes perfect. Just keep on practicing and I bet yours will look better every time you do it," I said easily.

Amy Courter

"Can I try next, Amber?" asked Beth. "I want to watch you do Lindsey's so I can try to do the same on Sophie."

"Then one more time after that," Sophie chipped in. "I want to watch somebody, so I know how to do a French braid, too."

"Yeah, but you have Amber to do yours," Lindsey said. "Our moms don't know how to French braid."

I saw Sophie smile and not say a word.

***

Rachel scooted her chair close to mine after church service Sunday night and said, "I hear you need to give me some lessons on French braiding!"

I smiled as I said, "The girls were such fun last night! Each one of them has a beautiful head of hair so braiding their hair was so easy. I will show you, but Lindsey is getting the hang of it. I bet she will be able to do her own French braid pretty darn soon!"

"It was good of you to have the three girls, Amber. I was a little concerned that Beth would be there when she had been so mean to Lindsey, but Lindsey said all that is forgotten now and there had been a misunderstanding."

Coffee, Anyone?

I smiled and nodded, "That's what I heard, too. I wish we could all be more like our girls and forgive and forget."

"True, that," Rachel commented.

Amy Courter

Chapter 20
Josh

This case I'm currently working is making me sick. We've been trying to catch these mother fuckers for three years now. Every time we get close, I'll think, we finally are going to be able to arrest these scumbags. But we get there too late, and they have already moved the girls. It's like they know when we are going to move on them, and they move before we do. It's so exasperating.

Last night we broke into the house where we had heard, through our source, they were keeping the girls in the basement, the restraints still dangling, and I swear I could still feel the body heat of the girls on the basement floor. We were that close to catching them! There was a baby doll in one corner left behind and one of the girls had written on the door with her fingernail, "HELP ME!" It just about broke my heart.

Coffee, Anyone?

Luckily, Eric and I have been on this same case and can talk through it when we want to, commiserating with each other, and sometimes when none of that works, we can just get shit-faced, drowning our sorrows with a bottle of scotch. Damn. There are so many fucking perverts out there. I can't even imagine what these poor girls go through, some as young as five or six. Even if we catch the shits who are the ringleaders, there are 100 more stepping up to take their place because the money they make on these girls is astronomical. Eric and I try to focus on busting and stopping ONE sex ring at a time.

The girls are stolen from various cities all over the country, but mostly outside of the United States in other countries. There are so many layers to a sex trafficking ring, which is probably why it is so hard to catch them. Nobody knows all the connections. Each layer knows only one guy or two outside their own layer and that keeps the other layers safe. If one layer of the trafficking is compromised, the ring can just replace that one section and keep the action going.

Amy Courter

Typically, it starts with a charming, good looking dude luring in a young girl who is alone at the mall, telling her how beautiful and pretty she is and can he help carry her package to her vehicle. It doesn't matter if she says no, because they have been watching her since she drove up alone and walked into the mall. They parked their tinted-window van right next to her car so that when she came back to her car, they could quickly grab the girl as she walks between their van with the sliding door and her car, knock her out with chloroform and drag her into their van in less than three seconds flat. You could blink your eyes and miss it. That's what they are counting on.

It's true what they say about the first 48 hours being the most crucial in finding a missing person. It's probably even less hours in a sex trafficking ring. The name of their game is moving the "merchandise" as quickly as they can to the next layer, each layer of filthy scum taking their fair share of the profit.

I've talked to some girls that we have rescued over the years, and they are not okay. I don't know if any amount of therapy will ever help them be okay. What these girls have had to endure just makes me sick. I think of my Sophie and Amber, and I just pray to God that they never have to experience anything remotely similar to this horrendous, vicious, sick scheme.

Coffee, Anyone?

Sometimes I want to tell Amber about this case and then I just can't do it. It's just too hard to talk about with someone that hasn't seen this stuff. How do you even explain any of it?! It's unimaginable. It's disgusting. It's sick. I've heard some of the names of past presidents and past government officials, lawyers, accountants, bank presidents who have all participated in this sick scheme. I'm filled with such rage. How could anyone want to hurt an innocent child like that.

Sometimes I dream of being on the other side of the law and becoming a hit man. I would take out these mother fuckers, one by one. They'd never see me coming. I wouldn't have to make sure I did everything by the book so that the charge would stick, I could just take them out then and there and be done with them. I smile a bitter smile.

About five years back we were able to intercept a group of girls being sold at the border. They had been smuggled over from Mexico in the bottom of a fishing boat. They were wet, sick, and confused. They thought they were coming to the United States to work in a restaurant. Unfortunately, we only caught the one guy running the boat and he wasn't talking.

Amy Courter

Another time, I was assigned to a case in Boston and after 10 months we were able to interrupt a human organ smuggling ring. We made our bust just seconds after a heart had been removed from a young Jamaican boy. Some days, it's just too much to think about.

I was thinking about the call from Nellie, my neighbor, a few months back. She acted like a crazy person! She told me I tricked her and that I "inferred" I was going to marry her. I can't believe she thought that! I would have never hired her to move in with Sophie if I had known she was such a bizarre broad. Sophie tried to tell me that Nellie was a nut on weekends when I was home, but I didn't listen.

Coffee, Anyone?

Maybe when I thanked Nellie for letting me know about Denise having an affair is where Nellie thought I "inferred" I was going to marry her. I was grateful to know it (well, not really) and encouraged Nellie to find out more. I told her to bake something, but not with nuts since Denise had a severe peanut allergy and have her over for coffee. I thought maybe Denise would tell Nellie more information I needed to know. I just wanted to be ready and aware of what was going on. I do remember Nellie making a very strange remark a few weeks afterwards, like, "Well, it didn't work. She's on a diet and wouldn't eat any." Or something like that! I remember being confused and saying, "What?!" Nellie really didn't answer me. I was in the middle of this big case at the time and was too busy to really think too much about what Nellie did or didn't mean by her remark.

Amy Courter

I suppose it didn't help when Nellie came to me in the middle of the night when I was home for a weekend shortly after I hired her to move in with Sophie while I was out of town for work. I saw her go home to her own house, so I thought she had gone to stay over there before I went to bed. I locked up the house and went to bed. She must have used the house key I gave her to get back in. I should have stopped myself when she climbed into my bed naked with her voluptuous body. At first, I didn't realize who it was since I had been sleeping, but I was awake enough at the end that I should have stopped. I didn't want to stop, though. It had been a very long time for me. I did tell Nellie afterwards that we shouldn't have done it especially with Sophie down the hall. I told her she needed to leave, and she did. It got kind of weird after that and I tried to avoid her whenever I could.

I got my house key back from Nellie after I told her she could move back to her own home when I married Amber. I remember her snarkily saying, "Oh, you're done with me now?"

***

I did a deep dive on the background of that kid, Jeremy. He isn't as suspicious as I thought he would be. Good student, good athlete. He was even homecoming king at his high school in Storm Lake. His parents seem like decent people, too. I will watch and wait, because I still feel like he is after something...

Coffee, Anyone?

Chapter 21
Amber

I was getting ready Saturday morning to drive to Ames to judge high school speech contests. Today is the Large Group State contest. I was asked to judge in Fort Dodge, but I didn't want to have it be awkward if one of Sophie's friends would be in my One Act Play category.

I've been trying to encourage Sophie and her friends to go out for drama and speech their freshman year and told them all the benefits that go with being able to stand up in front of a group and speak. They were not fascinated with any of it. Maybe next year, I hoped as I got in my car and backed out of the driveway.

I texted Jeremy this morning and told him what I was doing that day, since I would be in Ames and asked if he wanted to meet me for supper later. He surprised me by saying that he, too, was going to be judging at Ames High School today! I guess the apple doesn't fall far from the tree! That made me smile and choke up. I'm glad he inherited the adventure side of me, although I am sure his adopted parents had something to do with his adventure or boldness.

Amy Courter

Jeremy said he was out for speech and drama all four years of high school and made it to All State several times as well. His favorite category is Group Improvisation. I have never judged that category and I think it would be terrifying to draw a situation from three choices and two characters and figure it out in a five-minute prep time. They have to rely on other members of their team to be on the same wavelength as themselves. The objective is to create a scene using their situation and have it progress from point A to point B. That category is not for me, but I marvel at those that can do it and are good at it! We are going to see how our schedules line up and try to make lunch work at the school.

I saw some fantastic stuff today in One Act Plays and looked at my phone to see if Jeremy was done judging the morning groups; he was! I'm almost giddy walking down the hall to the Judge's Lunchroom. What a nice spread of food they have for us! All kinds of fruits to choose from, as well as lasagna and Texas toast. Yum. I worked up an appetite this morning! I grin at Jeremy as he starts filling his plate and I point to a table. He nods and I pick up my bottle of water on the way to my seat.

Jeremy slides into the chair beside me and bows his head for a quick prayer. I couldn't help it; tears rolled down my cheeks. "Jeremy, you are a Christian!" I choked out.

Coffee, Anyone?

"Yes, I have been for a while now, probably junior high age," Jeremy smiled at me.

"I'm so glad! It gives us another bond, loving the same Father God," I say.

"Yes, we have lots in common, I am learning," Jeremy says sparking a dimple. "I wish I could have judged a few weeks ago at large group district speech contests, but the rules say that new judges need to judge state contests first where there are three judges. I suppose that makes sense. That way a new inexperienced judge won't keep some group from going to state that really belongs there."

"Yes. I remember my first time judging at the state contest. I was a wreck, but I didn't have the experience YOU have where you participated all four years of high school in speech/drama, and you also had the privilege to go to All State!"

"Have you seen some good stuff today, Jeremy?" I ask as I forked a huge bite of lasagna into my mouth.

"I sure have! These guys are amazing! I have given out mostly '1s' this morning. There were only two that didn't get from Point A to Point B. I felt bad for them. But you can't give 1s to everyone or it wouldn't mean anything," Jeremy said with sympathetic eyes.

Amy Courter

"That's right. These kids work so hard at what they are doing, and I admire their strength and willingness to put themselves out there. Hopefully, our comments will help them to improve the category they chose and will help in the future to want them to try it again. That's what I worry about the most when I am judging. I want to encourage, encourage, encourage, even if I am giving them a 2 rating," I said.

"Yup. That's what I was taught, too," Jeremy responded.

"So, you got your certification after high school then, because you enjoyed it so much?" I questioned.

"Yes, I actually just got certified a few months ago. I was lucky to be able to do it in Ames and not have to drive 100 miles to find a center to get certified. I'm surprised you don't judge in Fort Dodge since it is closer," Jeremy responded.

"Yes, well, with Sophie being in high school, I didn't want to be the reason someone she knew and liked, did not do as well as they thought they should have, so I opted for an out-of-town contest center," I said.
"Oh, sure, I totally understand. Smart move, actually," Jeremy nodded.

"Are you judging in Des Moines for Individual District Speech in a few weeks?" I asked.

Coffee, Anyone?

"Yes, I'm judging at Hoover High School. I'm not sure of the category yet, though," Jeremy said as he bit into a shiny, red apple.

I started shaking my head hardly believing my ears. "Jeremy, I am judging there, too! How about if I pick you up on my way to Des Moines in a few weeks and we can ride together?"

"That would be awesome, Amber!" Jeremy smiled.

"I have to ask you, Jeremy, I noticed you took a bottle of water and there were so many sodas to choose from. Are you not a soda drinker?"

"Nope. Never have been. The fizz — carbonation, hurts my throat. I have never liked sodas. I drink a lot of milk, though. It's good for you, you know," Jeremy said with a wink.

"Ha!" I laughed. "I just wondered because I never liked soda either. One time when I was a kid my brother paid me a dime to take a sip of Pepsi just so he could watch my face while I drank it. It was putrid!"

Amy Courter

We laughed together and had yet another thing in common. It was time to get back to our assignments. I reluctantly got up from my chair and told Jeremy, "Have a good afternoon, Jeremy! I loved having lunch with you!"

"Me too, Amber!" Hope your afternoon is as good as your morning! If I don't see you before the end of the day, I will text you to let you know where to pick me up in a couple of weeks," Jeremy said as he put his empty plate in the garbage.

I walked to the restroom thanking God for this amazing young man and the opportunity to meet and get to know him.

***

"Are you kidding?" I texted incredulously. "So glad you got one of your favorite choices of Public Address! What are the chances of that?!"

"Slim to none most likely!" Jeremy responded by text.

"I've got the category, Original Oratory. Hey, we can study together on the way to Des Moines. You can ask the questions to me for the test we will be taking once we get there," I texted back.

"Sounds good to me. I really haven't had time to look at the questions, so that will help me know the answers by asking you the questions," Jeremy texted.

Coffee, Anyone?

"Okay, it's a date. I will pick you up outside of Maple Hall front entrance at 6:15 AM," I text back.

"See you on Saturday, Amber. Looking forward to it," Jeremy texts.

***

It was so much fun at the Individual District Speech contest at Hoover High School. They fed us so well all day long, although it was a very long day. I got Jeremy home about 7PM. We were too tired to even stop and eat. We just wanted to each get home and crash. Our brains were mush from seeing so many great speeches and writing encouraging comments on each of the ballots.

What a day. God is so good. And what a blessed girl I am to have this opportunity to meet and get to know this amazing son of mine. My heart is full.

Sophie had supper ready for me when I got home about 8PM. "Sophie, this is so sweet! How did you know I didn't eat supper?" I asked.

Sophie looked a little sheepish and said, "I texted Jeremy and asked."

"Oh!" I said surprised. "Is that the first time you have done that?" I asked.

Amy Courter

"Um. No. I wanted to get to know him, too, and I wanted to tell him about you since he missed out on having you as a parent. I thought maybe I could fill in some of the blanks for him since you are raising me," Sophie responded.

"Jeremy didn't tell me any of this," I said, puzzled. "I'm afraid your dad won't like this. He's had a hard enough time accepting that I am getting to know Jeremy, let alone you Sophie."

"I asked Jeremy not to tell you and that I would tell you myself," Sophie explained. "I know Dad would not appreciate me doing this, but I had to see for myself. As an only child, it's been fun to get to know more family."

"I understand, Sophie, but you probably need to tell your dad at some point," I winced."

"Yeah, I know," Sophie frowned. "I will do it soon."

"Meanwhile, what kind of sandwich did you make me here? It's looks delicious! And thank you so much for thinking of me! It was a grueling day!" I said, looking at Sophie.

"That's what Jeremy said, too!" Sophie laughed. "He said his bladder got VERY full because it was so busy, one group after another after another that he hardly had time to empty it!"

Coffee, Anyone?

"Oh boy, that's the awful truth," I said groaning. "My poor head. Des Moines schools have so many participants and to get them through the day, they work the judges to the bone. I think sometimes the bigger schools have trouble finding judges to go there and judge because of that fact. I would much rather judge in a smaller town with smaller numbers that space the day out a little better. I always feel like I'm behind before I hardly get started in the day in Des Moines, but they do what they have to do."

"You have my curiosity up with speech now that I know Jeremy does it too. I would really like to go with you next time just to see what kind of categories there are and what they do. Would you mind if I go with you to Individual State Speech contest in March? Jeremy told me there is one more contest left," Sophie said.

"Yes, Jeremy is correct. I have committed to an Individual State Speech Contest in Waukee, Iowa in March. It's over an hour away, though. We would have to leave before 6AM. Still want to come with me?"

"Yes! Is Jeremy doing that one, too?" Sophie asked innocently.

"Yes, he is. We are planning to carpool again. If you go with me, I will need to tell your dad."

Amy Courter

"That won't be fun, but yes, you are right," said Sophie.

***

I told Josh about Jeremy and the speech contests and even the soda. He was amazed. He said, "Who doesn't like soda?! That's ridiculous! Everybody likes soda!"

"Well, Jeremy and I do NOT!" I laughed.

I thought Josh would comment SOMETHING when I told him that Jeremy was a Christian, but he didn't say a word; he only raised his eyebrows in acknowledgement. I told Josh that Sophie asked if she could go with me to the next speech contest in March in Waukee. He was surprised to hear that, but I could tell he was pleased. Then I mentioned that we would be picking up Jeremy on the way to Waukee.

"Why does Jeremy have to go with you guys?" Josh countered.

"Why not? He is going to the same place we are, and I will be practically driving right by the university on my way. We might as well save him a couple bucks in gas by taking him with us."

"I suppose. I did do some investigating on Jeremy, and he APPEARS to be a pretty good kid, I guess," Josh reluctantly admitted.

Coffee, Anyone?

"Yes, I agree. Did you know he was homecoming king his senior year in high school in Storm Lake? The only reason I know this is because he told me he had to make a quick trip home in October to crown the new homecoming king, and then didn't get back home until Christmas," I said.

"He does seem pretty likeable," Josh nodded.

***

Wouldn't you know it's supposed to snow all day since it is speech contest day? Dang. I told Jeremy I would pick him up about 6:15AM in front of Maple Hall again. It is just snowing a little right now. Maybe the weatherman is wrong; he often is.

Sophie is up and ready and we didn't have enough snow yet to even scoop, so we are on our way. I am hoping I can just sit her beside us while we are taking tests before the contest starts and then we will just have her follow us to our assigned center so she can watch and enjoy.

"Hi, Sophie, it's nice to finally meet you face to face," Jeremy said as he scooted into the backseat of my Prius.

Amy Courter

"Yes, I agree, Jeremy, it's nice to meet you as well! I'm nervous about today and I don't even have to do anything, but this is my first time at one of these things and I don't know what to expect!" exclaimed Sophie.

Jeremy nodded and said, "You will have a great time today, Sophie. Here--I have an extra pad of paper. You can write on here what you think we should have given each person that we see and your reasons why, and we'll fill you in later to see if we judged them the same. I am in Center 3 all day with Spontaneous Speaking and your mom is in Center 6 with Storytelling. I'm going to walk with you to each of our centers so you know where to find us and you can just go back and forth between the two centers all day.
"Okay, but I don't know what I am doing," Sophie admitted.

"Not a problem; it's like getting free entertainment all day long! That's how I feel anyway!" Jeremy smiled.

"Me too, Jeremy," I nodded, thanking him for taking Sophie under his wing.

***

Coffee, Anyone?

I'm a little worried as we start home. It has been snowing all day long and there is at least a foot of snow on the ground. I can barely see the center line as I start driving northeast. Sophie and Jeremy are happily chatting away seemingly oblivious to the weather and talking about the contest and what did you give this one and what about her. Why did you give that one a 1 and that one a 2? It was interesting to listen, but I was trying to concentrate on staying on the road. Everyone driving in front of me was going very slowly, which was good. I just kept following the car in front of me since I could see their lights through the blowing snow.

Finally, the two of them came up for air and Jeremy said, "You know, my roommate went home this weekend, so if you two want to stay in my dorm room, you would each have a bed. I can sleep in the lounge down the hall. I feel like the snow is getting thicker and blowing harder and maybe you shouldn't try to drive the rest of the way home to Fort Dodge tonight in the dark. What are your thoughts?"

Amy Courter

So, Jeremy HAD been keeping an eye on the weather while simultaneously talking with Sophie and letting her know why he loved speech so much and why he gave this person this rating and that person another rating. I could see Sophie smiling like she liked that idea a LOT. And I must admit, I was terribly tense in driving the short distance to Ames from Waukee, so I relented and said, "Thank you, Jeremy. We will take you up on that. As soon as the roads are plowed in the morning, we will take off, but that is very kind of you to invite us."

"Good. We got that settled then," Jeremy said looking pleased with himself.

Jeremy took us to the girls' floor of his dorm, the floor above his floor, to use the bathroom and waited for us at the end of the hall. After Jeremy got us settled in his dorm room in Maple Hall, he showed me how to lock the door and showed me where he would be staying in case we needed him. He said he would have his cell phone with him and told me that Sophie and I would be safe in his room.

Coffee, Anyone?

The next morning there were a lot of drifts, but the snowplows had been out already and had made good progress by the time we were up and had gone over to the cafeteria with Jeremy for breakfast. By the time we had finished eating, I felt like we had a clear enough route to get back to Fort Dodge. I turned and thanked Jeremy and stepped closer to give him my first hug. I didn't want to let go. Sophie smiled at Jeremy and squeezed his hand and then folded into a hug with him herself.

"Go slow and turn around and come back if you need to," Jeremy said as Sophie and I walked out to my car. I waved and got the car going, heater full blast. Sophie got a scraper, too, and we made good time between the two of us, clearing off the ice and snow from the windshield.

"I really like Jeremy, Amber," Sophie said, looking at me sideways from the passenger seat.

"I like Jeremy, too, Sophie," I said and smiled. "That was quite the weekend, huh?"

"Yeah. Question for you: why did you clear the room after that girl got done telling her story?" Sophie asked as she glanced down at her pad of paper Jeremy had given her.

Amy Courter

"Oh, I was so sad about that one. One of the rules for Storytelling is that once you get up on the story telling stool to tell your story, you have to stay there. You can have a short introduction while standing by the stool and not yet get on the stool, but once you are up on the stool, you can't get down from it until you are done with your story. Unfortunately, I think the girl had a 'brain fart' and thought that pacing would help so she got down off the stool, and I had to disqualify her. I saw her climbing down and tried mental telepathy to tell her NO—DON'T GET DOWN! But it didn't work. Sometimes it happens, especially to newbies, where they get a little rattled. See, you are learning all this stuff now, so you won't make these mistakes next year when you go out for speech and drama!" I say with a grin.

"Did you like Jeremy's category of Spontaneous Speaking better than mine, Story Telling? I asked.

"No, there was so much more to have to come up with in Spontaneous Speaking and it seemed harder to me. I would rather do Story Telling probably since you can at least memorize it," Sophie said with a serious face.

"Well, there are other categories as well to choose from. I will show you when we get home and try to give you an example of each. I should have had you go to all the centers and see what area you liked the best, if I had been thinking," I said regretfully.

Coffee, Anyone?

"I actually did go to a couple other centers since Jeremy showed me how to get from his Center to yours and I knew I wouldn't get lost. I also watched a couple of performances in both Mime and Reviewing. They were interesting as well," Sophie said with a smile on her face.

"Well, look at you, all grown up and leaving the nest!" I reached over and ruffled her "feathers" playfully. I'm glad you felt confident enough to walk around a bit and look at some of the other categories. Maybe you can talk to some of your friends and get them involved as well. I am sure that Mrs. Marsden, the drama coach, would love to see more of you involved in speech next year," I said.

Sophie answered, "Yes, I plan to do that. It really helped talking to Jeremy about it on the way home. He told me how much speech helped him with other things all through high school and with job interviews, too. He said being able to express yourself clearly and effectively is one of the most important things you can do for yourself and your future."

Well said, Jeremy, I think with a smile. It's been a good couple of days, and I bet Sophie and I will both sleep well tonight. Fred, our fat cat, will be happy to see us; well, maybe not happy to see ME but happy to see Sophie!

Amy Courter

Josh wasn't crazy about us being on the road last night with the blinding, blowing snow and was very thankful we had a place to wait out the storm that was safe. I think Jeremy is growing on him.

Coffee, Anyone?

Chapter 22
Josh

Man, it's nice to be home and relax. It's kind of a trick of the trade to be able to compartmentalize my job from my home and family. I see such horrendous things in my job that I cannot just "unsee" so even though I can forget those things for a short while, they are never really gone from my memory. I am thankful for the here and now today! I can worry about tomorrow later.

I have to admit I have been very impressed with that kid, Jeremy, and offering his dorm room up to Sophie and Amber last weekend. That was very amazing that he thought about the weather and my girls driving home alone in the dark with the snow blowing and drifting so hard. Amber said she didn't even ask him; he just told the girls he had a room and beds for them both if they wanted them. Mr. Responsibility; he obviously has a big heart.

***

"What?! No coffee?!" I say under my breath. "Amber, don't we have any coffee, or did you move it somewhere else?" I ask as I keep poking under the cabinet where the coffee used to be.

Amy Courter

"You can try my brand if you like, Josh. It's Starbucks caramel in a sack. Do you see it? I forgot to pick up your brand at the store this week after you finished the last of it — sorry!"

"No, I don't like Starbucks and I don't like flavored coffee. It's too strong for me," I said. Ahh. Here is good ol' Folgers pushed way in the back. I open the can and it is only half full and has a weird aroma. "Smell this, Amber. What does that smell like to you?"

Amber sniffed, turned up her nose and said, "Not sure."

"Well, coffee doesn't actually spoil, does it?" I ask. "I think it just doesn't taste as fresh or strong maybe. Anyway, I am going to try a cup. Want some?"

"Uh, no thanks," Amber makes a face and leaves the room with the laundry basket on her hip.

"Good morning, sweet Sophie," I say as Sophie lazily stretches as she walks down the hallway in her pajamas and favorite canary yellow socks. "What are your plans for the day?" I ask as she sits at the counter bar while I am measuring out the last tablespoon of coffee.

"I dunno," Sophie mumbled. "Can I have some of that? Maybe it will help wake me up."

Coffee, Anyone?

"Sure. Although I don't know how good it will be. Smells a bit funky. It's probably just a tad old since it's been down there in the cupboard for over a year now, unless Nellie drank coffee," I remarked.

"Yeah, Nellie drinks coffee," Sophie said. "She brought over some coffee after Mom died and said Mom borrowed some coffee from her and she came to get it or something. She must have just walked in our house because I didn't hear her knock or anything. She just appeared in the kitchen. I think I surprised her."

"Hmmm. Weird. Nellie is an odd duck, isn't she?" I asked. Something was nagging at the back of my brain, but I couldn't quite grab it.

"Annnnd your coffee is ready, my lady, enjoy!" I said as I handed Sophie her cup of joe.
Taking my first sip, I tried to identify the flavor I was tasting. I couldn't put my finger on it, though. However, I did note that it was a little salty. There was something else, though. What is that taste?

I shrug and say, "I don't think the coffee will hurt you, Sophie, but I am definitely going to the store to get a new can of Folgers!"

Amy Courter

"Yea, Dad," Sophie says as she punches the air. After taking a shallow sip, she says, "I'll wait for the next brew, Dad — this one is nasty," and proceeded to dump it down the drain.

"Where are you going hon?" Amber asks as she is walking down the stairs to the kitchen.

"Need more coffee," I respond while putting on my coat. I think that last can got bad on us.

Amber opens the can again and sniffs. Then sniffs again and says, "Smells kind of like... peanuts to me." Digging with a spoon, she says, "Look, I even found part of a peanut in the bottom of the can. How did that get in here?"

I stop in my tracks, eyes wide, looking horrified. Sophie hadn't noticed and had already gone back to her room.

"What is it, Josh? Your eyes are scaring me!" Amber whispers.

"Amber...what if that can of coffee is the murder weapon?" Josh responds slowly.

"What? What are you talking about? Murder weapon for what or who?" Amber asks confused.

Coffee, Anyone?

"My wife, Denise, had a severe peanut allergy. You heard what Sophie just said about Nellie appearing in the kitchen out of nowhere with a coffee can in her hand shortly after Denise died," I said staring at Amber.

"Are you serious? Would Nellie DO something like that?" Amber asked in disbelief. "Why would she do that, Josh? What would her motive be?"

"I think she wanted ME," I said looking at my shoes.

"That's ridiculous!" Amber says shaking her head. "I mean, not that she would WANT you, but to actually KILL Denise to GET you?! I mean, COME ON!"

"Oh boy, let's sit down and talk this through. I'm afraid I may have encouraged some of this," I start to explain.

Amy Courter

"Nellie called me about a month or two before Denise died and told me that Denise confided in her that she was having an affair with her boss and Nellie thought I deserved to know the truth. I remembered being startled by that statement, although maybe I should have known it was coming since Denise and I had been fighting lately. I had absolutely no clue that she was having an affair, though; however, Denise did say she wanted to leave me. I said something to Nellie, like, "Try to find out more. Maybe bake something, but with no nuts. She has a severe peanut allergy. Have her over for coffee and maybe you can find out more."

"I don't understand, Josh. Why do you think you encouraged Nellie?" Amber asked.

"I'm not done yet," I said. "The following week Nellie called and said something like, 'It didn't work, she's on a diet so she didn't eat any,' or something like that and I remember thinking, What?? So now, what I am thinking is what if Nellie thought I meant the exact OPPOSITE of what I said, 'Don't make something with nuts since she has a severe peanut allergy' and took it upon herself to bake something WITH nuts in it hoping Denise would eat it and die, but Denise didn't eat any of it because she was dieting."

"Okay…I'm following you, I think, but this is crazy," Amber says. "Go on."

Coffee, Anyone?

"Okay, what if Nellie thinks well, I can't get her to eat the damn nuts so I will put the peanuts in the coffee grounds to roll around a bit to get the oil on the coffee grounds since I KNOW she likes and drinks coffee."

"Wouldn't the police have found this evidence, though, Josh?"

"Maybe not, Amber. Look at us, or me anyway. I couldn't figure out what the aroma or flavor is, and neither could Sophie. But maybe, just MAYBE Nellie had the can at her own house and after the police had combed our house Nellie brought the can here to our house making it look like I was the guilty one?"

"Oh no!" Amber gasped with her hand to her mouth.

Amy Courter

"Wait. There's more, unfortunately," I say. "I should have told you this, but I was ashamed of myself. After Denise died, I put an ad in the paper to see if I could find someone to be kind of a live-in nanny with Sophie while I was traveling. That person would get Sophie to school, her swim practice and meets, cook for her and just live here with her except on the weekends when I was home. I didn't get any takers, except for next-door-Nellie. She came over and said she saw my ad and she would like to have the job. I talked to Sophie, who wasn't very keen on that idea, but we both agreed that Mom would have probably liked that her friend, Nellie, would be helping us out, so Nellie moved in."

Coffee, Anyone?

"At first it was working out pretty well. Sophie didn't LOVE it, but Sophie didn't like a lot of things, being a teen and all. Anyway, one night, I saw Nellie leave and I thought she went back to her own house for the evening, so I locked up and went to bed myself. In the middle of the night, Nellie climbed into bed with me, NAKED! At first, I must have thought I was dreaming of Denise but at some point, I definitely knew who it was and what we were doing, but I didn't stop. It had been such a long time for me, and I am sad to say that I let my hormones take over. I did tell Nellie that I thought we should not have done it, especially with Sophie just down the hall. I asked her to leave, and she did. It was awkward for a while and then I thought we had both put it behind us. Except, when I told Nellie that I was marrying you about eight months later, she got all bent out of shape. I asked her for my housekey back and told her she could move back to her own house now and I would pay her an extra month's salary."

"Josh, it's understandable. She kind of tricked you. You thought she had gone home," Amber said, trying to let me off the hook.

Amy Courter

"Not quite done," I grimaced. "Anyway, after I told Nellie I was marrying you, she calls my cell phone several months later and tells me I hurt her feelings and she thought I was going to marry HER. I remember kind of snorting or maybe even laughing, although I didn't do it on purpose to hurt her, but said something like, 'I NEVER said I wanted to marry you, Nellie'. Then she told me that I 'inferred' it. There. That's all of it. After that, I blocked her number on my cell so she couldn't call me again."

"I see," said Amber. "Now what should we do?"

"Well, I just had an idea, but I will need to take what I think I know to the police and get their help," I said.

Coffee, Anyone?

Chapter 23
Maggie

"I just don't know how to help her, Amber," I sniffed as I confided in my friend and co-worker.

"I'm so sorry this is happening, Maggie. Do you know of anything that might be bothering Annie right now?"

"I can't think of anything. She has everything going for her. She's cute, funny, has a darling figure and both girls and boys like her. I don't understand why she is harming herself. Do you think if I hid all the knives in the house it would stop?" I ask.

"No, she would just find something else to cut with, like a paper clip, scissors or a razor blade. A knife is not the problem," Amber said sadly. I had a friend in high school that did self-harm and pulled out her hair by the roots. She finally had to wear a wig when she had a big bald spot on top."

"Ohmygosh. Why would anyone DO that?!" I exclaimed.

Amy Courter

"Well, why would anyone want to be bulimic or cut themselves? I think the professionals kind of put these all in a 'self-harm' category. Especially with young girls. What is Annie — 12 now?" Amber asked.

"Yes, she just turned 12 and has just started getting some curves to her body. Maybe it's scary for her and that's why she is cutting herself," I said.

"It could be. I think there are lots of different reasons young girls do this. Is there anybody you know that has been through something like this that could talk to her?" Amber asked.

Terrified, I ask, "Do you think this is about suicide and her wanting to actually end her life?"

"From what I have read and also from having a friend that did something similar, it isn't about suicide, although I suppose it could happen accidentally. It is more about needing a coping mechanism," Amber replied.

"But what could she be coping with?" I ask confused.

Coffee, Anyone?

Amber shrugged saying, "Maybe frustration, or anger, or even emotional pain. Articles have said that sometimes the pain of the cut or hair pulling takes away the emotional pain or anger or whatever is bothering the person and then there is relief or calmness, kind of like exchanging one pain for the pain that you don't know how to deal with."

"I'm so out of my element here I don't know where to turn for help," I said throwing up my arms.

"What about just having a conversation with Annie and see if she will talk to you about what's going on. Maybe she already knows she needs some help and will be open to talking to a professional," Amber suggested.

I slowly nodded, "It's a good place to start. I'll keep you in the loop. Has Sophie or her friends dealt with this sort of thing?"

Amber thought for a minute and then said, "Not that I know of, but I have only been in Sophie's life for a few months. I can ask her if you want me to, but if you don't want me to, I won't say a thing to Sophie. Just let me know how I can help."

Amy Courter

"You already have, friend, just by listening and letting me know other people have been through this. I am hoping your friend that pulled out her hair still has some hair left and got through her ordeal?" I asked hopefully.

"Yes, she did finally. I think it started out as a coping mechanism for frustration and then it got to be a habit. Her therapist suggested wearing a rubber band on each wrist and when she felt frustrated or angry and wanted to pull out her hair, she was supposed to snap the rubber band on her wrist. It kind of hurts, too! I tried it! The therapist also said that journaling would help so my friend did some of that, too."

"Oh, and one more thing my friend did that I think was helpful to her: our class had to write a research paper in high school, and she wrote hers on self-harming. Her mother even helped her with some of the research by reading a book or two on the subject and reported back to my friend. I think it helped them both to try to understand this condition. At least as much as you CAN understand it. She eventually quit doing it, whether she was outgrowing it or cured of it or just maturity, she just quit doing it one day."

I shook my head and said, "Growing up is NOT for sissies."

Coffee, Anyone?

"Totally agree with you on that, my friend. Hang in there. You and Annie have a good relationship and I am betting she will talk to you. Maybe not right away but I think she will talk to you eventually," Amber said with a hug.

Chapter 24
Josh

"Hi, Nellie, can I come in? I need to talk to you," I say with what I hope looks like concern and remorse.

Nellie coldly looks at me, as I stand at her back door then says, "Sure, why not."

"Oh, who do we have here? I don't remember you having a dog! He sure is cute and friendly!" I say with enthusiasm.

"I just got HER from the rescue place in town a few weeks ago. She is just a mutt, but she is able to help me with the lonelies," Nellie says as she reaches down to scoop the little jumping live-wire up in her arms.

"What's her name?" I ask.

"Gert. Short for Gertrude," Nellie responds.

"Haven't heard that name in a while," I say laughing while scratching Gert behind her ears.

"Why are you here, and where's your 'FAMILY', Josh?" Nellie asks with a cruel smile.

Coffee, Anyone?

"Amber and Sophie are shopping today, and I just thought this might be a good time to talk. Nellie, I am SO sorry the way I treated you after Denise died. I was not in a good place. You were nothing but kind to Sophie and me. I don't know WHAT we would have done if you had not moved in with Sophie while I was working out of town. You fed her, did laundry, cleaned the house, cooked for her and got her to school and activities every day. I owe you a huge apology. Will you forgive me, please, Nellie?" I sincerely ask.

Nellie just looks at me for several seconds and I can't tell what she is thinking. Finally, she nods and says, "You WERE a pretty big jerk. And you are right, I was a Godsend. You would not have found ANYBODY to move in and keep house for you and your bratty daughter. You took almost a full year out of my life, you know. A year wasted. And for what? You hardly even thanked me for stepping in to bail you out in your time of need. Last time I'll do THAT for anybody again."

"You are so right, Nellie. I WAS a terrible jerk, and I would like to make it up to you," I said with a caring face.

"And how do you plan to do that?" asked Nellie, still with some attitude.

Amy Courter

"Well, for starters, can I offer you a $1,000," I say as I pull out my wallet. "And I would also like to have my guy take care of your lawn in the summer and your driveway and walk in the winter, if you will accept that as well."

Nellie's facial expression does not change, but she says, "Alright. I will accept both your money and lawn and driveway clearance. Thank you. It's just nice to be appreciated. I thought you just forgot all about me once you had your sights set on Amber and it really hurt me."

"Yeah, well I'm afraid Amber and I are not going to make it," I say with a furrowed brow while lying through my teeth. "I shouldn't have rushed into that marriage so quickly. I think I was just infatuated with her and could not see her faults. She is a very selfish, self-centered person and I just did not realize it until too late."

"Gee, that's too bad," Nellie half smiled. "I want to say, 'I told you so' but I won't since you appear to be struggling."

"Right," I say looking down at my shoes. "I should have seen what a good thing I had right in front of me, but I must have been blind."

I move forward with my hand to caress Nellie's face, but she stops me and takes a step backwards.

Coffee, Anyone?

"Not so fast, Mr. Prince Charming," she says wagging her finger at me. "You don't just get to trade one model in for another when you don't like what you chose."

"Oh, of course, I'm sorry," I grovel. "You just look so beautiful with your hair down like that and holding cute little Gert. I got carried away for a quick second. Friends, then, Nellie?" I ask holding out my hand.

"Yes, we can be friends, Josh," she says shaking my hand. And thank you for doing right by me with the cash and the hiring of my lawn and drive. I do appreciate your efforts there. May I ask for one more thing? I will need some help every now and then for someone to take care of Gert when I am not home. It wouldn't be very often, but I don't know anyone else that I trust to do that for me."

"I know for a fact that Sophie and Amber would love to do that when I am out of town, and I will do my share if I am home as well. We would be honored to do that for you, Nellie. Gert looks like such a fun little girl." Then I add, "Amber has been begging to add a dog to our family for months now so I know she would love to have Gert over whenever you need someone to watch her."

Nellie smiled and said, "Thank you."

Amy Courter

I smile looking at Nellie and say, "You are very welcome, Nellie. I'm sorry I made you feel unappreciated. I'm not good at acknowledgement. Denise was always telling me that I really fall short there."

At Denise's name, Nellie's mouth turned downward, and she said, "Well, Denise wasn't very good at showing HER appreciation for a good man when she had one, so don't feel TOO bad about it."

Feeling more hopeful when I heard Nellie's remark about Denise, I continued. "We were yelling and fighting a lot at the end of Denise's life. I wish we could have worked it out, but when you told me she was having an affair, I just didn't think it was going to be possible," I said sadly.

"I get it, Josh, I really do, but why didn't you just divorce her," Nellie asked puzzled.

"It really hadn't gotten to that point yet. We were not getting along, but she hadn't actually ASKED for a divorce although she had said she WANTED to leave. I just thought maybe we could try to work through it, but then she died."

"You mean, she died with a 'little help' don't you?" Nellie questioned looking me straight in the eye.

Coffee, Anyone?

"Wh..at??" I said slowly, trying to figure out the direction we are heading.

"Come on, Josh, I'm not stupid. Denise carried that EpiPen with her wherever she went. Why would she not have used it? You and I both know what happened to Denise, DON'T we, Josh?" Nellie said, pushing her chin in the air.

Okay she is admitting it. Tread carefully now, I say to myself. "Yes, I think we both know what really happened to Denise, Nellie. It's very sad, but I do understand why you did it. You had your eye on the prize and…," I stop because Nellie's eyes are wide with disbelief, and she interrupts.

"What the hell, Josh! I DID NOT KILL DENISE — YOU DID!!" Nellie yells at me while shaking her finger in my face.

"What are you talking about, Nellie? I told you about Denise's peanut allergy and then shortly after that she dies from drinking coffee that has peanuts rolling around in the grounds!" YOU did THAT!" I yelled back.

Amy Courter

"Denise told me herself about her peanut allergy. I already knew about it, Josh. Is THAT how you killed her? I wasn't sure until just now how you did it, only that I was not going to rat on you, knowing that she did the unforgiveable to you. I just felt like it was justice for you; however, later when you were shutting me out of your life, I did wish I had told the police what I suspected."

"Wait. What about the day you 'popped up' at our house and Sophie saw you with the coffee can? She said she thought she startled you and you looked guilty. Why were you in our kitchen and with a coffee can?" I asked staring at her.

"Just like I told Sophie, I wanted my coffee back. Denise had asked me for some coffee the morning before she died—she couldn't find hers, and I just gave her my can of Maxwell House coffee, thinking she would take out what she needed and bring it back. When she didn't return it, and I realize it was because she died, I decided to just go over and get it myself a few days later. I did notice there was another can of coffee--HER brand of Folgers, when I took mine from your cupboard, which was interesting to me that she borrowed coffee from me when she had some of her own."

Coffee, Anyone?

"This is crazy, Nellie! I didn't kill her. You thought I killed Denise and I thought YOU killed Denise!" I say astonished. If you didn't put the peanuts in the coffee can to kill her and I didn't do it, who the heck did?"

We look at each other silently, our minds going the same direction, but thinking, oh hell, no!

Amy Courter

Chapter 25
Amber

I've been worried about Maggie and her daughter, Annie, and hope they can get the help they need. Mags told me I could share Annie's cutting situation with Sophie, and after telling Sophie about little Annie, she asked if she could invite Maggie and Annie to church with us. Bob works nights, so he wouldn't be able to come. We are also picking up Sophie's old friend, Beth, and taking her with us tonight for church. I've got a full load in my little Prius.

Coffee, Anyone?

The youth group at our church is second to none. I don't know where they found the youth pastor, but he is amazing. He has several of the youth lead worship before the Sunday night service begins with guitars, tambourines, drums and wow, can the group sing! It blesses me so much to see Sophie up there singing along, her face shining, and seeing such peace in her soul. She seems like a different girl than the one I met several months ago. I smile to myself; that's because she IS a different girl than the one I met several months ago. Sophie has been reading her new teen Bible with "the Help" in the margins and has been asking me lots of questions. But mostly, I see her ponder what she has read. I know she is getting very close to making a commitment. I'm not rushing her. In His time…

Chapter 26
Police Chief Knoll

Well, that didn't go as planned, thought Police Chief Knoll. When Josh Jackson came to us recently with his "theory" that his live-in nanny may have killed his wife over a year ago, it sounded pretty bazaar, but I was willing to give him the benefit of the doubt and let him try wearing the wire he suggested while talking to the nanny, his next-door neighbor. He assured me that he did this kind of thing all the time in his job. I have to admit that after listening to the recording of their exchange, Josh Jackson played his part in the "sting operation" very well. He is a very good actor. If the neighbor had been the killer, she would have cracked or admitted it to him. There was no reason for her to lie to him; she didn't know he was wearing a wire. Instead, she thought she was letting him off the hook and that he now has justification for what the wife did to him. She thought Josh did it and was going to let him get by with it and not tell us a thing!

Coffee, Anyone?

Now we are back where we started, however, now it appears to have been a homicide that we didn't address. I really wanted to continue the investigation further last year, but the mayor, Jim Jante, my boss, told me to let it go since we had investigated the husband and found no fault there. So, I closed the case and now I wish I had pushed back a little harder with my boss; after all, it was HIS administrative assistant who died for Pete's sake! I remember thinking it odd that Mayor Jante even called me about the case last year when Denise Jackson died and told me to wrap it up and be done with it. He said her family had grieved enough without this continuing investigation that was clearly NOT a homicide. Usually, the mayor does not get involved in our cases for the most part.

Amy Courter

I really wanted to interview the daughter, Sophie. When we questioned the husband, Joshua, about the empty Reese's Peanut Butter Cup wrapper that we had found in a big garbage sack near Denise in the kitchen, he was adamant about us not interviewing Sophie. He said neither he or Sophie buy or eat peanuts or peanut butter just to be safe around Denise since she has an extreme peanut allergy. He did say that it may have come from one of Sophie's friends and the friend had possibly put the wrapper in Sophie's garbage upstairs. The father was worried about the possible guilt Sophie may feel if one of her friends was responsible for the death of her mother. Since Denise appeared to be in the process of collecting garbage from all over the house with her big garbage bag, it did seem possible. We found her lying in a mess of spilled coffee on the floor with a dumped, wet and soggy purse, apparently looking for her EpiPen, which still has not been located.

Coffee, Anyone?

I remember interrogating Nellie, the neighbor, last year and thinking there was something she was not telling me. It might have been her shifty eyes or her haughtiness, but something was definitely off. She just didn't act like someone that was innocent of any wrongdoing. She was one of the "persons of interest" I wanted to re-investigate before my boss told me to leave it alone. I want to re-open the case, but I am not going to tell my boss just yet. Due to his interference in making us close the case before we were able to interview all persons of interest, we did a very inept, shoddy investigation.

I now have the suspect coffee can with the deadly peanut and peanut oil in the grounds. I'll have my team discreetly check for fingerprints on the can, although Josh had admitted to at least his and maybe his new wife's prints possibly being on the can since he just discovered the peanut-coffee can pushed back in the cupboard.

Amy Courter

Chapter 27
Sophie

Youth group was so cool Sunday night. We had sharing and prayer time where people could talk about anything bothering them and then we would all pray about it. I was so surprised that little Annie confessed to her cutting and said she would like some prayers to stop doing it. I told her afterwards that she was a very brave girl and that she can call me any time she feels the urge to hurt herself. My friend, Bradley gave her a hug afterwards, followed by my other friends. Essentially, our whole youth group is a very non-judgmental group and I think Annie felt the comfort in that.

I've been talking a lot to Jeremy through texting but haven't told Amber and Dad about it. Well, I guess I did tell them both about texting Jeremy earlier when he and Amber were doing speech contests together, but I don't think they know we have been having continued conversations through texting.

Jeremy has such faith! I was so surprised when I was telling him about Amber's friend Maggie and her daughter, Annie. Jeremy said he would pray for her. When I thanked him, he asked me if I had anything I wanted him to pray about as well. Then he told me he has been praying for our family ever since he met us!

Coffee, Anyone?

Jeremy is so easy to talk to and I can tell he will not tell anybody, not even Amber, what we talk about. I feel like he really IS my big brother; okay, stepbrother if I have to get technical, but still…

Chapter 28
Amber

The other day I was talking to Jeremy. He is busy getting ready for finals, but said it is so noisy in the dorm and that's it's hard to find a quiet spot to settle down and focus. He has been using the library on campus but said he gets tired of sitting in that hard chair for hours, plus it closes eventually, and sometimes he studies into the wee hours of the night. I had an idea but need to run it by Josh first.

We have this big 4-bedroom, 2-story old Victorian home and why not see if Jeremy would like to come and stay with us for a few days so he can study in a quiet space. The house is empty after we all leave for work or school, so he could just spread out or stay in a bedroom, whatever he wants. Ames is not that far from Fort Dodge to drive back and forth for a few days. He said he only has one test each day and has already taken one of the finals. It would be fun having him here even if he is busy studying. I haven't even asked Jeremy if he would WANT to come and stay with us so he can study quietly, so he may not even want to do that. I need to check with Josh first, though, to see how he feels.

***

Coffee, Anyone?

Josh wore his wire the other day when Sophie and I were shopping and told me later that Nellie didn't kill Denise. I said, "How do you know for sure?"

Josh said with a laugh, "It was kind of funny, actually. Nellie thought I killed Denise and was actually going to let me get away with it because Denise 'deserved' it because she had an affair! Can you imagine that?!"

"Well, that sounds like she DID do it if she thinks Denise deserved to die, I think."

"No, trust me, she didn't do it. Hey, did you know Nellie got a new little mutt? Her name is Gert and she is so cute!"

"Joshua Jackson! You are softening, aren't you?! Are you saying we can get a dog for our family now?"

"Whoa. Settle down. Not so fast! However, I did volunteer us all to take care of Nellie's cute little Gert if she is away from home for any length of time."

"So, your wire-wearing didn't upset Nellie and now you two are friends?" I asked incredulously.

Amy Courter

Josh snorted and said, "I never told Nellie that I was trying to get her to confess. I suppose I need to do that sometime, because I thought I was going to have to pretend to seduce her and make out with her in order to get the truth, so I told her you and I weren't getting along and told her she was so beautiful. I think she saw right through me. I do need to tell her the truth sometime."

"Right. Because we don't want her to get the wrong idea! And you are MINE, I said as I reached up for a kiss and hug. Do you often seduce women to get to the truth?" I ask with an arched eyebrow.

Josh laughed and said, "Only YOU!" Changing the subject, he said, "So now I need to go back to Police Chief Knoll and talk about what was said on the wire and figure out our next step or if she will even let me HELP with the next step. She may want to handle it by herself."

"Oh, Police Chief Knoll is a woman?" I asked.

"Yes, but don't let her gender fool you; she sure knows her stuff. Tough as nails!" Josh said with a nod.

Coffee, Anyone?

Chapter 29
Jim Jante (Mayor)

I saw Josh Jackson leaving the Police Station the other day when I was going home for lunch. What, I wonder, is that all about? I will have to ask Police Chief Knoll next time we have our 1:1 briefing.

I miss my administrative assistant, Denise terribly. She was such an encourager to me. She constantly stroked my ego and made me feel like a million bucks. Too bad she had to die.

Amy Courter

We were doing so well as a couple, discreet and completely off anyone's radar. We agreed to tell no one. With her husband out of town so often, and my wife being the social butterfly that she is, it was perfect. I always parked inside Denise's garage and even though my whole vehicle wouldn't fit in there, nobody could see it from the street. I thought I could go on like that forever. Until we couldn't. Why did Denise have to pressure me saying we both needed to leave our marriages and marry each other? There is no way in hell I would do that. My wife has ties to the government with her dear old dad being a Senator. My chances of re-election would go right down the tubes if I dumped his only darling daughter. So, Denise left me no choice. She was threatening to expose our affair and I couldn't have that.

Coffee, Anyone?

I had to very meticulously develop a plan and carry out the scheme to the letter. There was no room for error. I took a full can of Planter's peanuts and shook them into a half-full coffee can that I had taken from Denise's home and even let it "marinate" overnight after shaking it around furiously for a full minute. The next day I took my wife's noodle strainer and was able to sift out the peanuts, leaving the coffee grounds in the coffee can, along with the peanut oil on the grounds. I thought it was ingenious of me to think of this plan, I smiled rubbing my hands together as I drove over to Denise's house. I had my own key to let myself in and put the Folger's coffee can back in the cupboard. Since she was at our office working, I knew I wouldn't get caught. When leaving Denise at the office, I just told her I was running some errands and would be back.

Amy Courter

I knew Denise would go to her EpiPen immediately when she started having trouble breathing after drinking the peanut-tainted coffee. The EpiPen is never far from her, so one night I slipped it out of her purse and took it home with me. I took the chance that she had an extra EpiPen somewhere else close by, but I didn't know where to look for it and was hoping it would be far enough away that she wouldn't make it to the other location (if she had one) of the EpiPen in time. Well, it worked, obviously! But I AM sad that I will have to look for a new Administrative Assistant. She was a good one, both at the office and in bed, I smile to myself. I've had a temp from the agency for the past year, but she seems happily married and too "business-like", so she is a no. I'll keep looking.

Coffee, Anyone?

Chapter 30
Police Chief Knoll

Josh Jackson is right. There are numerous fingerprints on the coffee can, but so very interesting to me are the fingerprints I found that should NOT be on there. I will have to be very careful in pursuing this murder investigation and I need more than just his fingerprints on the coffee can since it doesn't identify him 100% to be the killer. I need something else as well. I need to go back to the neighbor, Nellie, and interview her again.

Amy Courter

Chapter 31
Josh

Amber asked me if I would mind if she invited Jeremy, her biological son to our place for a few days so he can study in peace and quiet for his finals. The more Amber tells me about this kid, Jeremy, the more I like the dude. He seems so laid back, easy going, yet ready to tackle the world. Not your typical freshman in college, that's for sure.

Sophie told me a few months ago that she and Jeremy had texted a few times when Amber and Josh were doing speech contests together. I can hardly believe the change in Sophie since I married Amber. Sophie was such a surly, volatile girl after Denise's death and now I see the peace and contentment on her face and in her actions, too. Sophie even offered to do the prayer before supper the other night. Her prayer was not one she found in a book; I could tell. It was from her heart and when I looked up at her after the prayer, she had tears in her eyes. I did too. This girl. She is special. And I think I have Amber to thank for this change and maybe the God she talks about all the time.

Coffee, Anyone?

I would not have believed I would have felt this way or wanted this several months back, but I am looking forward to having Jeremy stay with us for a bit. He is just what I would have loved and wanted in a son, if I had had a son, that is.

Chapter 32
Jeremy

Wow. Amber has invited me to her house for the week if I want to come and study in peace and quiet with no interruptions. I am pretty stoked about that. I was thinking about making the long trip home to Storm Lake to get some peace and quiet so I could really just focus on studying for my finals, but this will be the next best thing, plus a good chance to get to know Amber and her family better.

Amber would have made a good mom, but I totally understand why she did what she did at 18 years old. According to Sophie, Amber IS a good mom. Sophie's latest text was asking me what I thought of her calling Amber "Mom". I told her to follow her heart.

I remember going through a stage, about age seven or eight when my adoptive parents told me that I was adopted. I felt unwanted and unloved since my "real" mom did not want me. My parents sat me down and explained how unselfish my biological mother was in going through with the pregnancy at such a young age. They told me she had written a note that went along with the adoption, "To the Adoptive Parents: Please take good care of this baby boy and love him with all your heart. It's all I ask of you."

Coffee, Anyone?

My parents told me that and said I was the best gift they had ever received in their lives. I still remember that day. They are the kindest, most loving parents a guy could have, and I told myself that several times throughout my life already.

And now I feel I have the best of both worlds and have also been able to meet my biological mother and love her as well. I think I will take Amber up on her offer to come and stay in Fort Dodge with the Jackson family. I'm looking forward to it.

Chapter 33
Police Chief Knoll

"Hello, Nellie Namanny?" I asked when she answered the door.

"Yes, that's me. What's the problem officer?"

"I need to clear up a few things with the Denise Jackson death from last year. Do you have a couple of minutes to talk with me about that?" I asked as I pushed her door open a little further.

"Well, I am supposed to be working, but sure, I can take a 10-minute break. What's on your mind?" she asked.

"Do you remember seeing any vehicles at Denise's house the day that she died? More specifically, that morning or even the day before?"

"Josh told me you might be contacting me about Denise's death. And just to be transparent, I did not kill Denise."

Coffee, Anyone?

"No, I do not suspect you, Ms. Namanny, but I do have some concerns that I may have closed this case too soon. Can you help me with any vehicles that you may have seen come or go between the day before and the day of Denise's death?"

"As a matter of fact, I do remember a black Audi SQ8. I remember because that is not a common vehicle," Nellie said with confidence.

Nodding I said, "No, it certainly is not! Probably a $90,000 vehicle I'm guessing. Do you know who that vehicle belongs to, by chance?"

"I do know that the vehicle is at the house quite often but usually he parks it in the garage, hanging out it just a bit. Denise always told me that when that vehicle is at her house and in her garage, do NOT come over," Nellie said with a smirk.

"Oh, did we have some hanky-panky going on?" I ask with raised eyebrows.

"Yes, I would say so, although I do not know the person's name; however, I do have the license plate number I copied down," Nellie says. "Let me go get it. Oh, and this little jumping bean is Gert. You can pick her up if you want. She LOVES people!"

Amy Courter

"Hi, Gert! You sure are a cutie!" I say while scratching under Gert's chin, small as it is. "Just thinking, how did you know if this vehicle was in the garage and not to come over when it was in the garage?"

Nellie's voice for another room said, "His vehicle doesn't quite fit in the garage so a little bit of it always stuck out and he had to leave the garage door open. Nobody can see the vehicle from the street, only me, the neighbor."

"Ahh." I say.

Nellie returned with a piece of paper in her hand, "Here it is. I was about to take my morning walk when the Audi pulled into Denise's drive. He was only in the house for a short time. I would say less than a minute and like I said, he usually parks in the garage. He had something under his arm."

"Was Denise home when this person stopped over?"

"No, she was at work, I assumed. She always left about 7:45AM, first dropping Sophie at school and then driving on to work. The guy had a key to her door because Denise always locks her door."

Coffee, Anyone?

"Ahh. I see," I said, feeling very hopeful, while pocketing the license plate number. "You have been very helpful, Ms. Namanny. Thank you so much. I'll be on my way now. I am leaving you my card in case you think of anything else that might be pertinent to that time period," I say as I turn to leave.

"You're welcome. Hope you can nail him," Nellie calls as I am walking back to my vehicle.

I drive to the mayor's office and park behind his black Audi SQ8. I take the piece of paper with the license plate number out of my pocket and sure enough. It's the same license number. But is it enough?

Amy Courter

Chapter 34
Jim Jante (Mayor)

"Send her in, Alice," I say as I finish stacking my work on a corner of my desk so I can focus on my conversation with Police Chief Knoll.

I stand to shake her hand and study her face. She is a tough one to read and she sure doesn't wear her emotions on her sleeve.

"Good morning, Police Chief Knoll. What brings you by this lovely spring day?"

"I have a couple questions I'd like to run by you, sir. I had some new information brought to me regarding the Denise Jackson death and I need to re-open the case."

"What?!" I exclaim. "That was a long time ago, over a year! Why are we opening a closed case when we have so many open cases we should be working on, Chief? I thought I told you to close it. Is that why you had Josh Jackson in your office a couple of weeks ago? Why are you wasting valuable time on a closed case, Chief?"

"Like I said, new information has been brought to light that we now need to investigate further."

Coffee, Anyone?

"What new information?" I demanded.

"Sir, have you ever been to Denise Jackson's home?" she asks.

"Now why would I do that, Chief? She was my employee. I NEVER went to her house, and I can't believe you just asked me that. How inappropriate."

"All the same, I need to ask these questions to clear some things up so I can close the case again. You were never at the Jackson's house for any reason: a birthday party, a dinner, or anything else, correct?"

"That's correct, dammit, do I have to say it twice, Chief?" I yell, my face turning red.

"Sir, your fingerprints were found on the murder weapon inside Denise Jackson's home."

"That's IMPOSSIBLE!" I say panicking minute by minute. "Wait, didn't she die of a peanut allergy? How could my fingerprints be on anything?" I ask starting to sweat profusely.

Amy Courter

"Here's the thing," said Police Chief Knoll. "It appears that Denise Jackson was murdered by someone close to her that knew about her peanut allergy and tainted her coffee can by shaking up some peanuts in the coffee grounds, and then removing them, knowing she would drink the tainted coffee. It's just a miracle we were able to uncover this!"

"I don't know what that has to do with me, Chief," I say with a gulp, loosening my tie.

"Oh, I think you really do know, sir. In fact, I am guessing that the reason you are sweating so heavily is because you are as guilty as sin. We also have a witness that saw you the morning before her death, drive into the Jackson driveway, using a key to unlock her door. You came back outside less than a minute later, just enough time to put a tainted coffee can in a cupboard where you knew Denise would see it and use it the next morning."

"How DARE you! I have never heard some rubbish. Now get the hell out of my office! Don't you ever show your face here again—YOU ARE FIRED!" I yell standing up.

Coffee, Anyone?

As Police Chief Knoll leaves my office, slamming the door behind her, my head is pounding. Why did I not tie up the loose ends and get the coffee can out of the house, I think to myself. How could I have been so stupid? Think. Think. Think. How can I turn this around? Nobody will believe the Chief's word against mine. But, just in case, maybe I should follow her to see where she goes. I can't have her telling anyone else about this.

Chapter 35
Josh

"He's on the move, guys," I say into the FBI radio transmitter as the mayor practically rips out his transmission by putting the gear from reverse to drive without a stop in-between. "Do NOT lose him!" I say as I pull into traffic with a vehicle between the mayor and me.

He's flying through yellow lights and red ones, too. I continue to pursue him, knowing that Police Chief Knoll's life depends on it. I am hoping she sticks to the plan and drives home like we discussed. That's where I have two of my FBI team waiting for the mayor. I am guessing he is really getting desperate and hasn't even noticed me following him yet. He is so intent on catching the Chief that he can hardly see what's in front of him let alone in back of him.

Oh no! The mayor is catching up to the Chief and he is riding her tail like there is no tomorrow!

"Change of plans, guys," I say into my radio. "I need you on the corner of 15th and 2nd Street South pronto. Looks like she isn't going to make it home before he tries to run her off the road. I'm still on his tail and have my gun out and ready, just in case."

Coffee, Anyone?

Now the mayor is slamming into her vehicle and trying to push her in it. My heart is slamming in my chest. I'm trying to stay calm. Damn. Where is an officer when you need one?! If she would just pull over, I could take it from there, but she keeps driving and taking corner after corner like a Nascar driver. Damn, she's good, I think shaking my head.

Shit, he is shooting at her now! Time to end this fiasco. "Okay guys, we have our proof. Close in and keep your weapons ready," I say as I smash into his vehicle from behind. Another FBI agent pulls up beside him; another in front. We've got him. It looks like his air bag (and mine) inflated and he is motionless.

I get out of my vehicle carefully with my gun pointed at the mayor's vehicle, circling around until I am at the passenger side. The glass in the window is gone so I stick my gun through the window as the mayor slowly blinks and say, "You are under arrest for the murder of Denise Jackson. You have the right to remain silent…" I continue with his Miranda rights as one of the agents pull him out of his car and handcuff him, putting him in the backseat of their vehicle.

Amy Courter

Police Chief Knoll walks over to me, her face full of relief. "I wasn't sure it would work, baiting him like that. I was lucky he didn't ask for my gun and badge when he fired me. I didn't have to use my gun, but just the same, I was very glad I had it with me just in case," she said with huge eyes. "Thanks to your team, it's over," she said with gratitude.

"Yeah. And one more nail in his coffin—we got a warrant to search his office after he left it to tail you and we found an EpiPen in his desk drawer. We put him in the back seat but he's not saying anything, except "I want my lawyer!" Not that I blame him for not talking. He's going down for a very long time," I say shaking my head.

Coffee, Anyone?

Chapter 36
Jeremy

"I hear there was some excitement in your town recently," I say with a smile.

"Yes, that's an understatement," Josh nods.

"Good job in catching the mayor. That was quite a piece written in the *Fort Dodge Messenger*!"

"Thanks, but the real glory goes to Police Chief Knoll. She put her job and life on the line. She is one kick-ass woman! Did you know they want to promote her to the mayor of Fort Dodge now?"

I smile and say, "She deserves it. On another note, I sure do appreciate you opening your home to me so I can get some quiet study time."

Josh says, "Hey, I remember living in the dorms. Not a good place to study well or sleep well. I recall finding a spot at an all-night 'Denny's' back in my day when studying for my finals. I ended up paying a fortune in coffee, though, while I was there all night!"

"Hadn't thought of going there!"

Amy Courter

"Well, you don't have to since you have us," Josh said stretching out his fist for a fist bump. "Just pick out your room upstairs. There are two empty bedrooms, so we don't care which one you choose. And of course, you will eat meals with us. In the meantime, though, please make yourself at home."

"Will do, and thanks!" I say picking up my bag and turning toward the stairs.

"Don't mention it!" Josh calls over his shoulder.

Coffee, Anyone?

Chapter 37
Amber

Mags and I finally got our new Starbucks plugged into our Fort Dodge hotel after months of red tape with the process, which is great, but wouldn't you know it, the smell of my once-upon-a-time favorite drink just gags me now. Ick.

This is the second day in a row that I've lost my cookies right after breakfast. I have felt like this once before about 19 years ago. I know what is going on — I'm pregnant. Josh is going to be so upset with me. We haven't talked babies in several months and I pretty much forgot about it with all that we had going on here, but now, ready or not we are going to be parents again.

Amy Courter

Chapter 38
Josh

Big changes in our family! I resigned from the FBI and took a job offer from the Division of Criminal Investigation (DCI). I will have an office out of Fort Dodge. It will be so nice to be able to spend most of my evenings in Fort Dodge now instead of Georgetown. I will miss Erin though. He and I have great comradery. I think seeing the daily horror that we both experience and being able to talk through it together has helped keep me sane throughout my years on the force. But having time with Amber and Sophie and now our new little one will be well worth it. I miss them a lot and miss OUT on a lot when I am out of town for work. I may even start going to church with the girls now that I can. I am thinking there may be something to this Christianity thing.

Police Chief Knoll mentioned she is taking the mayor interim position and will probably run for mayor next election as well. When I told her about my new job, and about Erin and how we discussed the horrible stuff we had seen together and how I will miss that outlet, Chief said she could be that person for me since she likes a sounding board as well and has seen some pretty gruesome stuff herself.

Coffee, Anyone?

Six Months Later

Chapter 39
Sophie

"I have a new SIIIIIISSTA I say as I dance around my friend Lindsey's bedroom! I am so excited to have another sibling! You don't know what it's like being an only child. NOT FUN!"

"Oh, I don't know about that," said Lindsey skeptically. "I wouldn't mind getting rid of my little brother every now and then. He is so annoying!"

I laughed and said, "Oh, just be thankful for the little twerp!"

"Yeah, I am," she said. "MOST of the time! Plus, I need someone else to blame things on once in a while—ha ha!"

"Did you know that Amber and Dad asked Jeremy and me to be the baby's Godparents?" I asked with a huge grin on my face.

"Oh! That's so cool, Sophie!"

Amy Courter

"Yeah, Jeremy and I are pretty stoked about it. We'll have to show little Gretchen the ropes, you know and how to be a Christian."

"Wait. Did you...? Are you...?" she asks before she grabs me and hugs the heck out of me.

"YES!" I screamed, hugging her back. "I'm a Christian now, 100% sure! Between you and Jeremy and Amber, I have had good teachers and examples to follow. I took my time and read a lot of scripture. I was trying to make it so hard when actually, being a Christian is so simple. You either accept the gift of salvation God gives us in his Son, Jesus or you don't. Period. And I accepted and repented and here I am," I said with arms outstretched.

Lindsey moved in for another hug and said, "I'm so happy now, I'm crying. But good tears, Soph, good tears."

"You are not wiping your boogers on my shoulder, are you, girl?" I asked laughing.

"Uhhh...maybe just one!" she joked. "So, the baby's name is Gretchen, huh?"

"Yes, my dad said it's a 'kick butt' kinda name. It's the Police Chief's first name that helped catch my mom's killer."

Coffee, Anyone?

"Makes sense to name her that then!" she said. "Let's go find your baby sister. Maybe she needs fed or rocked or something."

As we walk over to my house, I am feeling so very thankful for the people in my life, and mostly for letting God into my life and Jesus into my heart. I can't imagine going through life without Him now.

As I open the baby's bedroom door and see Amber rocking baby Gretchen, I said, "Mom, can I please hold her?"

"Yes, you certainly can, daughter," she smiles warmly at me.

"Well, I need to practice calling you Mom since baby Gretchen will do that one day and I don't want her to get confused."

"I totally agree with you. We don't want to confuse little Gretchen," my mom said grinning ear to ear.

Amy Courter

Acknowledgements

I would like to thank my biggest cheerleader and best buddy, Mary (Petey) Smith who walked and talked with me throughout the process of writing my first book. She was a constant encourager telling me I could do it and believed in me every step of the way. She was my sounding board and inspiration, giving me ideas as well as letting me bounce ideas off her. Next, I would like to thank my daughter Stacy, the grammar police and editor, for her wonderful help in perusing my fiction novel and cheering me on. Finally, I would like to thank my husband, Kim, for his patience in my writing and help in the area of what a FBI agent may see or experience and my daughter, Sara, for her timely encouragement when I was stuck for a two-week period writing nothing. Thanks for reading my novel. I enjoyed writing every single chapter. I hope you enjoy reading it.

Book 2, *Sophie's Story* will be coming out shortly, a sequel to *Coffee, Anyone?*

Made in the USA
Middletown, DE
10 November 2022

14591418R00115